# HELP ME, RHONDA
# & OTHER STORIES

GUERNICA WORLD EDITIONS 23

# HELP ME, RHONDA
## & OTHER STORIES

P. David Hornik

GUERNICA
World
EDITIONS

TORONTO—BUFFALO—LANCASTER (U.K.)
2019

Michael Mirolla, editor
Cover design: Allen Jomoc, Jr.
Interior design: Jill Ronsley, suneditwrite.com
Guernica Editions Inc.
1569 Heritage Way, Oakville (ON), Canada L6M 2Z7
2250 Military Road, Tonawanda, N.Y. 14150-6000 U.S.A.
www.guernicaeditions.com

Distributors:
University of Toronto Press Distribution
5201 Dufferin Street, Toronto (ON), Canada M3H 5T8
Gazelle Book Services, White Cross Mills
High Town, Lancaster LA1 4XS U.K.

First edition.
Printed in Canada.

Legal Deposit—Third Quarter
Library of Congress Catalog Card Number: 2019930817
Library and Archives Canada Cataloguing in Publication
Title: Help me, Rhonda & other stories / P. David Hornik.
Other titles: Short stories. Selections | Help me, Rhonda and other stories
Names: Hornik, P. David, 1954- author.
Series: Guernica world editions ; 23.
Description: Series statement: Guernica world editions ; 23
Identifiers: Canadiana (print) 20190053046 |
Canadiana (ebook) 20190053070 | ISBN 9781771834636 (softcover) |
ISBN 9781771834643 (EPUB) | ISBN 9781771834650 (Kindle)
Classification: LCC PS3608.O676 A6 2019 | DDC 813/.6—dc23

*To Tami*

# Contents

# She's Not Here Now

EVERY TIME, THAT spring, I looked out my window into the city, I thought of Tara. I thought how strange it was that, even though I'd lived in or near the city for eleven years, she was the only person in it—in the country, for that matter—with whom I had, or possibly had, some connection.

That wasn't strictly true—there was also my wife; but my wife didn't count anymore, since we'd divorced the preceding November. And there were also the couples we'd known while still married; now, though, I felt I'd already lost the connections with these people.

So I would look, from my high window in the north of the city, down into the soft cream-gold and red of the center of the city, and think how somewhere, in that soft mass of buildings, the mite that was Tara existed—she was there.

## 2

She'd come here from Vancouver. I'd met her in February, when it was still only trying to be spring. I was walking on Ben Yehuda Street; there was a competition between the sun and thick grey clouds, the stones of the street were damp, it was only an excuse for spring but people were milling about as if it had already arrived. I saw her, a woman with long blond hair, in a faded denim jacket and jeans, playing her guitar. Though never the type to introduce myself to a strange woman, in this case it seemed unpardonable not to.

Whereabouts in Canada? Vancouver. Toronto, too. Mostly Vancouver. That's really nice, what you play. Thank you. I've always liked that kind of music. Oh, really? Yes. I used to play piano ...

# 3

She was thirty-seven. A year ago, in Vancouver, she was supposed to get married—at last, never had before; but instead she and the man had broken up. Since then she'd been drifting—Yellow Knife, Santa Fe, Mexico City—but always with the idea in her mind of Jerusalem. Why Jerusalem? She couldn't say. As if it was both too obvious and too obscure.

In March it was already outdoor-café weather; she claimed this was all she had time for. She had a waitressing job long into the night; she picked up additional spare change playing guitar on Ben Yehuda. She was living in a hostel. The faded denim jacket and jeans were, I came to realize, practically her only clothes, aside from a few T-shirts.

She had a small face, with round features, and at worst could look pallid and pinched. Other times, though, with the shiny blond hair and a certain round candor of her eyes, she had some attractiveness. Her talk was slow and faltering, with long, bewildered pauses; I can't imagine anymore how I sustained as much conversation with her as I did.

Of course, I wouldn't have persisted in meeting with her if I hadn't been in a faltering, bewildered condition myself. At that stage I saw myself as little more than driftwood, hoping to graze another piece of driftwood in the stream. Also, she was interesting.

# 4

She grew up in a town on the coast quite a ways north of Vancouver. Her parents were immigrants—father from Trinidad, mother from Ireland; and she had five siblings. It was a fishing town, and her father was a fisherman. All in all it was a harsh, strained existence.

Her father, once, took her with him in his fishing boat. They came to a place where they could no longer see the shore; she felt scared, thrilled. Then she saw the net plunge into the water and come up filled with wriggling fish that flashed and sparkled in the sun. Her father poured the fish out on the deck, and it was if the sun had shattered onto the deck in glittering fragments.

# 5

In winter the sea turned grey and frigid, the days were short, and people spent their time cooped up together indoors. That, for her, was the worst of it. In childhood it didn't faze her; she and her friends would run outside and play in the snow. But in adolescence … that was when she started playing guitar.

Which, in itself, was a bitter struggle: She shared her room with two sisters and it could be an ordeal to wait till they weren't there, or to get them to let her play while they *were* there. Was she influenced, I asked, by the Canadian songsters—Ian and Sylvia, Joni Mitchell, Gordon Lightfoot? I was surprised when she answered that she didn't know them much then; she listened to the Beatles and the Rolling Stones, but not to them. She didn't have to listen to them, she explained—she was one of them.

I told her how, in around that era when I was growing up in northern New York State, I had a special fondness for those Canadian songsters; their guitar chords took me to dreamy places. I didn't tell her that, when I first saw her playing guitar on Ben Yehuda, I almost felt I was back in one of those places.

She didn't go to college, but she went to Vancouver and worked as a musician, waitress, barmaid, secretary, sales clerk, switchboard operator. She had boyfriends, was supposed to get married a couple of times but nothing worked out. She went with one of them to Toronto for a while. About three years ago, back in Vancouver, she met Roger—and that was supposed to be it, she thought she'd finally settle down.

# 6

But why Jerusalem? I asked again.

It was April. We sat at a table under a canopy; around us was sunlight, patterns of leaves on pavement.

I hadn't seen her in a while. She'd turned down my previous couple of suggestions of meetings, talking about her time problems; yet something in her voice made me feel she wasn't just putting me off, or at least that it wasn't that simple.

Another thing that kept her on my mind—increasingly, and today more than ever—was the way she looked. She had a light golden tan now, and aside from being admirable in itself, it set off the yellow hair, making it more striking. Also, she'd managed to buy one new article of clothing—a red T-shirt. I'm pretty sure she was wearing it that day; it also fit into the picture well.

Why? She said.

I said: Yes, why. You're not Jewish, and I gather you're not a very observant Catholic. So …

She gave a look of round, vague perplexity.

Because I'm a lost soul.

Aren't lost souls supposed to come to Jerusalem?

# 7

That spring I was something of a lost soul myself, though it wouldn't have occurred to me that living in Jerusalem was a solution for it. I was alone—implacably so. Half a year ago I'd left my wife; a year before that my mother had died; fifteen years before that, my father, and also, somewhere in there, I'd left the country I'd grown up in. "Get thee out of thy country, and from thy kindred, and from thy father's house, unto a land that I will shew thee." "Therefore shall a man leave his father and his mother, and shall cleave unto his wife: and they shall be one flesh." These words, in terms of the leave-takings they dealt with, were certainly apt; but other words would have been needed to describe where I now felt I was.

And yet, compared to Tara, it was solid ground, it was security. Whether or not I would ever be in a family again, I had *been* in one, and remained the father of my children whom I saw every week. But Tara … Once she was a girl in British Columbia, I'd think, lying in my bed at night. A girl with shiny blond hair, living along the Pacific … what had happened to her since then? Anchorless, unable to hold onto anything?

I had nothing to do but think, and I thought long thoughts. About how, just at this time of my life when I was the most adrift I'd ever been, I'd met someone who was *more* adrift. How, just when I felt the most severed from my past I'd ever felt, I'd met someone who was like a stray, northern fragment of that past. How her hair still kept that gleam of northern sun.

8

The city, at dusk, was so soft and vague it could have dissolved and floated away. Birds—wing spans, rather, dark against silver—floated in the ambience. There were "buildings" out there, but far and faint, as if borderline-real.

My life. This is where I am, in my life. A long time ago people who are now dead conceived me; I dutifully took shape, assumed my form, walked, looked around and tried to make out what I was seeing.

Late April. Light falls in a late April dusk, bounces gently off roofs and pine trees, lands and is still. Birds seem weightless, stranded in ether …

Yes, but why not call her?

Call her?

Yes. So she hasn't returned your calls for two weeks—is that a reason not to call her? Did you expect her to be anything but tenuous, evasive …?

I walked out to the room I called my living room, where there was no light on and it was almost night. I didn't turn the light on. I went to the phone and dialed in the near-dark.

And again the voice from the hostel: She's not here now. Yes, I gave her your message. I don't know … I don't know.

# Driving South

OUTSIDE THE DARKNESS, the perfect, warm, silent darkness, a voice—a voice—a voice—he opened his eyes. He squinted— bright curtains in relief against the dusky room. A film of sweat on his neck. Traces of a dream he had just left—something about a girl, but he couldn't remember it ...

"*Ronnie!*"

"Coming," he droned. He swung his feet over the side of the bed and stiffly stood up; his body, which had been mostly idle this sum-mer, seemed to creak mournfully and complain. He pushed the door open, trudged out into the breezeway, up the steps into the kitchen where his mother was standing.

"You called me?" he said.

"Ronnie. What were you, asleep?"

"Yeah."

"It's such a nice day. Don't you want to go swimming?"

He shrugged. "I don't know."

"Would you do me a nice favor and pick up some things at the store for me?"

"Can't Allen do it?"

"Allen's very busy. Please Ronnie be a good boy and help out a little. Then maybe when you come back you can go for a swim."

ON HIS WAY to the driveway he passed Allen, his older brother. He was supposedly studying for his entrance exams or something like that. He saw him, stretched out on his back in a lawn chair, an angelic expression on his sleeping face.

He climbed into the old, stuffy Studebaker. It was always stuffy—the window on the right side went down only a few inches, not to mention the dank smell it kept even if anyone bothered taking it to a car wash. It was an ugly dark green, rusty and dented; but now it was "his" car—which meant they didn't want *him* driving the Impala. It sounded ready to die when he started it.

He drove past the cornfields that stretched off into hazy distance. The day was motionless. The sun glared down. He came to a straight, open stretch of road; ground his foot on the gas, watched the needle as the old wreck grumbled up to sixty, sixty-five, seventy. Even that, not such a thrill anymore. It had all been a thrill, just a few months ago, when he'd at last gotten his license. But now it was mostly errands—Ronnie, go get this, Ronnie, go get that.

In the cool supermarket he saw girls in halters and shorts, casually strolling around, checking prices. "Guys without girlfriends," his friend Phil had said, "they can look, but they can't touch." He saw one bend way over to take something out of the frozen case.

Then out in the parking lot it seemed far hotter than before, like a wall of heat. He walked past puddles of spilled oil that sparkled in the sunlight.

## 2

Back in his room, he sat on the edge of his bed leafing through a telephone book, gazing abstractedly at names of parents of girls whom he knew vaguely in school. It might not have been as bad this summer, but his best friend, Phil, was spending it at some vacation cottage with his family ... He eventually settled on a number; walked out to the breezeway where the telephone was.

"Hello? Is Randy around? ... Hello, Randy? Hi, it's Ron."

"Oh, hey, Ron, how you doin'. Haven't seen you in a while."

"Pretty good. How's your summer going?"

"Not bad. Workin' my ass off, but, what the hell."

"Where?"

"Huh?"

"What job have you got?"

"Oh, just washin' dishes over at Waggoner's. It busts your ass, but, what the hell, hah, hah, hah."

"Yeah. Listen, feel like goin' out tonight, playin' some basketball or something?"

"Tonight? Uh, let's see. Tonight … goin' to a party, over at Deb Smith's."

"Oh yeah?"

"Yeah. Wanna come? Supposed to be a keg of beer, hah, hah, hah."

"Nah, don't think so."

"Why not?"

"Well … I don't really know Deb. Got any other nights free this week?"

"Nope. Tonight's my night off."

"Oh. All right. Well, I'll probably see you one of these days, then."

"Yup. Take it easy, Ron."

"So long."

He hung up the phone, stretched, and stood there.

A yellow vase by the phone was lucent in sunlight.

Go down to the courts to play some basketball?

No, probably no one there. Too hot.

He found his father sitting up on the deck of the upright pool, reading the newspaper.

He stood behind the deck.

"Hey, dad, have you got any books I might want to read?"

His father turned, slightly startled, and looked at him. "What? You want books?"

"Well, I had nothing to do, and … I don't know …"

"Sure, all right." He elaborately took off his glasses, crushed a ciga-rette, put the newspaper aside, and stood up.

As they walked back to the house, feet moving in unison on thick grass, his father said: "Nice day today, why don't you go for a swim?"

"Nah, I don't really feel like it."

In the breezeway his father stood with his arms folded, surveying the shelves. He leaned over and took out a book.

"Ever read *Crime and Punishment*?"

"No. When was it written?"

"What? When?" He shrugged. "Nineteenth century, late nineteenth century."

"Oh. I think I'd prefer something more recent."

He gazed at the book a moment longer; then put it back.

He searched ... "Want to read a novel by John O'Hara?"

He pulled a paperback halfway from the shelf. Ron glanced at the cover and saw a woman in a low-cut dress.

"When was it written?"

"This? Nineteen-forties, I think."

"Oh. Nah, I guess I'll try *Crime and Punishment*."

But sitting in the living room with the book, he was soon discouraged. He suffered with the long names he couldn't keep track of, the endless paragraphs. All he'd wanted was a fast-moving book in simple language with a lot of quick dialogue.

He set the book down after a few pages. He gazed emptily out the window at the road and the fields beyond it, then at the clock on the mantelpiece. Four o'clock. What was the date, something like July 17?—fourteen days left in July, how many in August, thirty?—about forty-five days left to the summer, that meant. Forty-five days. His mother had suggested getting a job; he really didn't know how to go about it ... But there was always the coming school year. One girl— that was all it took. You only had to get to know one of them. He'd be looser, more easy-going this year. He'd walk right up to girls and talk to them.

"Oh no ... Ronnie!"

"Yeah ..."

"Ronnie!"

"Yeah!"

"Why did you get hot dog rolls? Didn't I say hamburger rolls?"

"Damn it ..."

"It's all right. We'll just … we'll have them plain."

He sat there in the room.

"Nah, it's all right!" he called. "Mom, it's all right! I'll go back to the store!"

# 3

Again he passed his brother in the lawn chair. This time he was on his side, head slouched on a limp arm, mouth wide open.

The day hadn't changed much. The sun, if a little lower, was as fiercely hot and bright over the fields. He turned on a rock station. The dashboard was flooded with booming bass and thudding drums; above it all a voice screamed out in a frenzy. Sometimes it seemed that rock singers were the only people who understood him. He egged and harried the car to an almost savage speed; wind whipped in and flung his hair about. When he came to the road that led to the supermarket, he decided to turn the other way instead and take a short ride. He'd never driven this way before, but he had the impression there was a view of the river out there. Besides, it would kill time.

He soon found himself in a greener area; the flat fields gave way to low, grassy hills and patches of trees. He passed elegant white houses with wells and fences in their front yards. Trees lining the road cast pleasant shade across the car. He wondered if he'd get lost. As long as he stayed on this road it should be OK. It wouldn't matter if he came home late; he'd think of some excuse. Listening to the thumping rock songs and enjoying the wind, the light-shade, light-shade on his arms, he started to feel almost cheerful.

He came to an intersection where the road ended. He had to go right or left, or turn back. He seemed to remember having been here once before—was it in Phil's car?—and that there was a view of the river nearby. But which way? With his dim sense of direction he calculated that the river would be south of his house, therefore to the right. Without exactly deciding to, he turned right and drove on.

The country around him grew steadily wilder and prettier; soon there were no more houses to be seen. He passed a sign that said: SLOW—WINDING ROAD and another: WATCH FOR DEER. The Studebaker under his hands and right foot seemed amazingly light and smooth. He glanced at his wrist for his watch and saw, in surprise, that it wasn't there—he must have left it at home; well, if he didn't come to the river soon, he'd turn back.

The rock song that was on the radio began to blur and distort with loud bursts of static. He fooled with the tuning knob—it didn't help. The static grew louder and more persistent, till the music was almost drowned out. But just as he was about to turn off the radio he heard something else, apparently another station, coming in over the noise. Gradually the rock sounds and the static were displaced by a slow, sweet orchestral music with a harp thrumming pensive chords in the background. He was puzzled to find that he liked it. Was this one of those cheap, phony adult stations? He hadn't known they played such music.

He drove on absorbed in the music, his whole mood seeming to slow and blend with it. The car felt almost feathery as it gracefully swung around curves and skipped over bumps; all around him now were wooded hills and valleys. Then the song ended; or changed; and a new, even prettier theme replaced the other, this one even more slow and thoughtful, yet somehow joyous. He'd never known such music existed; immersed in it, he sank into a deep lassitude.

… He blinked, sat up straight. The song had ended, and the radio was silent. A subtle change seemed to have occurred within him; he felt oddly confident, at ease. Then he saw that the road had changed also—from grey concrete to yellow dirt, and that the car, which apparently had kept going while he was dozing, was moving along it at a mild pace. He wondered—though with only moderate curiosity—where he was. And what was that now, looming up ahead?—there seemed to be some long, low white buildings up there about half a mile off; grassy yards, clustered trees. Drawing nearer, he saw what seemed to be tractors and sheds, chicken coops or something off beyond the buildings. And now as cool shade closed over the car, and the scene ahead brightened, he made out that there were people—kids his own age it seemed, standing in a group on the left side of the road—turned toward him, almost as if they were waiting for him …

The car inched along up to them. Yes, they really were kids his own age—boys as well as girls—wearing jeans, T-shirts, shorts. All looking at him, though none seemed especially surprised or curious.

He pensively went on the brake; turned off the motor.

"Hi," said a tall, red-haired boy standing just outside the window.

"Hey, there," Ron said, leaning on an elbow.

"What's yer name?" the red-haired boy asked.

"Ron."

"Pleased to meet you, Ron. I'm Jeff. Why don't you come out and meet the rest of us?"

"OK. Sure." He climbed out of the car into cool, early evening air. There were about twenty of them, standing around the car. The boys seemed easy-going and friendly; the girls were all pretty and seemed eager to meet him. No one made him tense by being too forcefully genial.

"Long ride?" said another boy.

"Yeah," Ron said, glancing back at his car. "Where am I—where is this place?"

"A farm," said a third boy. "This is our farm."

"We were just trying to start up a basketball game," said Jeff. "Like basketball?"

"Yeah, sure."

"Give him a chance, Jeff, he must be tired," said one of the girls. Ron looked at her. She had brown skin, silky blond hair combed back from her forehead, blue, intelligent eyes the color of the sky in good weather … "My name's Clara. Why don't you come over and relax for a while."

"OK," Ron said.

"Feel like playing some basketball later, just come on down," said Jeff.

"OK. Sure," Ron said.

He followed her along a walkway. A nice, cool smell of grass, evening. Off in the distance, a red sun sinking into dim hills. Unlike the other girls, she was wearing a dress, a slight, white one; he watched her smooth brown calves.

She led him into what seemed like her own compartment of one of the low white buildings. Through a small living room into an even smaller room with a shaggy blue rug, mattress, yellow curtains with a beam of last sun filtering through.

"So, do you like it?" she said, turning to look at him with her calm eyes.

Later, Ron stepped out into the lawn. It was almost dark out; his skin tingled to a soft night breeze. A few stars flickered overhead; the sounds of a basketball game drifted over from nearby. His whole body felt vibrant with confident energy.

"Hey, Ron."

He turned; someone was sitting there under a tree. Ron went up; it was one of the boys he'd met earlier, leaning on his elbows with a beer bottle in his hand. "Hi," Ron said. "Sure is a nice evening."

"Sure is. You oughta go over to the court. I'm takin' a beer break. My team's one man down."

"Sure, OK," Ron said. A thought detained him. "By the way, do you know where my car went?"

"Your car?" The other boy peered ahead toward the road. "Nope. I don't know what happened to it, to tell you the truth."

Ron didn't say anything.

"Why? You got anywhere to go?"

Ron looked down at him.

"No," he said. "Guess not ... I think I'll stay right here."

# Thin Ice

*(a cycle of short fictions)*

## 1. *The Lifeguard in Autumn*

THE BEST THING about Sun Hill Apartments is the pool. The children's section is mercifully separate, and if you go early or late enough you stand a good chance of getting the grownups' section to yourself. Or, if you're too lazy for that, you can just sit by the redwood fence under the maples, sunk in a chair with a book, as worried about time as the leaves fluttering over your head. The din from the pool sounds soft and distant, through chinks in the fence you see summer fields languid in the heat.

In September it breaks. A cold wind bellows in; the startled air skulks off to hide. The oasis closes for the season: Its water is drained, its leaves erupt in glory, but the empty pool will soon be clogged with the colors. The time when you floated in evening water, drifting through shade and sunlight, is already consigned to the past.

I like to go for walks in September. With the children off to school, the fathers off to work, the mothers off to work, the place is as good as deserted. You can observe the silent life of birds and squirrels; your mind feels a little alien, dislodged, but at least it's your own.

I was surprised the first time I saw her. I've always liked to stand gazing at the blue cement pool after the season's over. I was planning to do that one day; but a surprise awaited me.

In a chair to one side of the pool—I'd just gone up and leaned my arms on the gate—a girl was sitting.

She was the lifeguard. I knew her from summer, a silent, shy young thing who had very little to do besides hang around and pretend to check IDs. She'd give me faint Hi's and Byes when I got there early or left late. But what was she doing here now? Did she have last-minute chores to finish? But why would she just be sitting, in her usual spot a little back from the children's section, seemingly doing nothing at all? And why, now that I noticed it, was she wearing only her blue bathing suit with a sweatshirt over it—as if it was still a summer morning?

I had to say something. We'd seen each other; it was too quiet to stay quiet.

I said: "Nice day for a tan."

She laughed—nervous and short.

"Still work here?"

She folded her hands on her stomach, nodded—not turning her head, faintly smiling.

"Well," I said, "don't work too hard."

I turned away, unsettled; I stalked off down the path with a sense that things were awry and had not been corrected.

In October, the season is still autumn, but the feeling is already winter. The birds are mostly gone. The mornings have a dazed clarity, as if they know what has happened but are still bewildered by it. Twilight is strange and soundless, grim with too much knowledge. I go for even more walks in October—that's something else I like, yellow leaves in green grass.

I had a sixth sense about it as I was going up the path; but then I thought, that's foolishness. And then, again, the sixth sense. The office building was on my right, the red and yellow maples on my left: I went up the three steps to the gate, leaned and rested my forearms: and there she was.

She might not have moved since September.

The curve of hair over her shoulder swung as she turned to look at me.

"Afternoon," I said.

She said "Hi" as her eyes moved away.

"Pretty cold out."

That got nothing, so I said: "Aren't you getting cold?"

She sat there, sunk in herself. "No."

I glanced at her bare legs.

"What are you doing out here?"

"Just"—she moved faintly—"guarding the pool."

I glanced at the pool: an empty pit, leaves stuck to the sides.

I said: "From what?

"I don't know."

"The season's over, isn't it?"

"Yeah."

"Then what are you guarding it from?"

"I don't know."

She was staring down at her playing hands.

"Well," I said. "Good luck."

She might have smiled.

Again I had to walk away. Whatever needed to be said hadn't been; nothing was right, and I had to leave it that way.

In November I stood at the fence, watching her pace back and forth on the pavement, barefoot and shivering, swinging her fists; I tried to get her to listen to me.

"You don't have to stay here anymore. It's off season. No one's coming. There's nothing to guard it from. Estelle (I remembered her name from the summer), do you know what the temperature is out here? It isn't even forty. You're going to get sick if you keep this up. You don't—you can't stay out here like this. Listen. Let me go home and get a pair of my wife's jeans—she's about your size—let me go home and get some jeans, and then at least you'll be covered. Better yet, we'll put you up for a while. You can use the extra room—it's no trouble. You could take it easy for a while ..."

The wind caught my words, whipped them around like leaves. There was a mood of alarm in the air, crows cawing, the year closing up. The pool area was desolate, the maples black against the sharp

November blue. Estelle paced back and forth, her eyes on the ground, not seeming to listen; I stood at the fence, gesturing, trying to reason with her.

A FEW DAYS later it snowed. There was over a foot by morning. I looked out the window and saw a bright desert; I realized that the sudden quiet of September, the dazed clarity of October, even the rush and alarm of November had been part of a revolt—against this, against the signs that soon it would just be this.

I went out. The sky was one white cloud; it seemed one could float into it. No path to the pool—I had to make one. She wasn't there. Her world was snow, her pool a white crater in the white. She left, I told myself, she's finally come to her senses.

I walked away and didn't look for her.

## 2. West of the Pond

Time dies late in the afternoon. Work is finished; you have no plans. It was beautiful when the sun set: You watched it from your warm room, how it died in a yellow glare over grey trees that already knew it was dusk and were ignoring it. Dusk; the children are on the pond; you have no plans.

Walking past the pond, you wish you could do what they can do. To swerve like that, to glide over the long grey glaze of frozen water … You stay well back from the shore, so they'll only see a shadow.

West of the pond it's already night in the woods. You walk till the clicks of sticks and pucks are only a far-off music, a mist of percussion over a lake of stillness. You stand; you let it become night in yourself.

The mood of the day is gone; this is what is left.

This is where the sun would have fallen. You saw it sink, how it caught its death of cold in a yellow blaze. But only its absence is left in these woods.

ONE GREY WEDNESDAY in November, the pond had frozen, really frozen, and Jo and I were the first to take advantage. She scampered onto the ice, slipped and tumbled, but started right up again. She loved this ice-skating, she said. I objected: It's not ice-skating, we're wearing boots, you have to wear ice-skates to ice-skate, a special kind of shoe. But she went on calling it ice-skating. Crows cawed from bare trees along the shore. Although, underfoot, the ice felt solid, I couldn't help thinking of falling. It never crossed Jo's mind. Of course, someone who weighs one-sixty is much more likely to go through.

DEEP IN THE woods, deeper than you could go (you had, after all, a home—people in it waiting for you), a pool of light seeps slowly into the snow. The frozen branches flare in it; but not for long. Soon it will go all the way down; then there will only be night and the icy stars.

## 3. *The Outlier*

Wesley hung around Colucca's with the regulars till midnight or so; after they left, he stayed at the bar until Lucky put his mop away, closed up the register and said: "Lights out, Wes." That was hours ago; but Wesley is still hanging around.

He's given up trying to understand her; but he keeps walking. Hands down in his pockets, head down toward the sidewalk. The winter night decreed a curfew on sound and movement; a few cold, bright stars keep watch.

Wesley, my cousin, has worked in the same car-repair shop, forty-five hours a week, fifty-one weeks a year, since he got out of high school more than a decade ago. He's an outlier; with his tall, stooped frame, morose eyes, often bad complexion, people don't take much account of him. Yet Wesley has his own peculiar, inner world of intense feelings. Though outwardly accepting of his plain life, he never really settled for it. He spent his free time bored, brooding—a hulking shape amid the noise at Colucca's; or—an even deeper refuge—at home listening to favorite songs, a secret world of emotion and truth. Candy Thinnes hit his life like a bombshell.

There was no real lead-up to it, no expectation, and no real reason for it. True, he would watch her at the roller rink he went to on weekends to kill the boredom. He liked the sleek look she still had even though, clearly, the years had taken a toll on her; and her somewhat bucktoothed smile, which guys he knew at work or at Colucca's, guys who thought about baseball and horses all the time, wouldn't have given a second glance—gave *him* a sensation like a tsunami. But it was only that—watching; he didn't think anything of it, that anything would ever come of it.

But he met her. Not by his intention, or hers; it just happened one day at the rink, maybe from their both being there a lot. What amazed him—it was something he could neither believe nor deny—was how much she seemed to like him. Movies with Candy, suppers at Candy's house (amid the babbling kids), nights in Candy's bed. He felt himself changing so fast he couldn't keep up with it. He spent the hours at the garage sweetly dreaming, like a high school kid …

That was summer. When fall came, and she went back to her job teaching at an elementary school and had less time, Wesley grew anxious. He'd look at her with slow, searching doubt: Had he been just a summer fling for her, an admirer to have around her at the rink? On September 27, without ever having mentioned the subject, he offered her an engagement ring, which she accepted.

I FOUND OUT about this from my mother, who found out about it from my aunt, Wesley's mother:

In November Candy broke off the engagement. One night Wesley stayed late at Colucca's. When he left, he didn't go home; he kept walking in the streets.

He found his way to where Candy's car was parked outside her house. It was a freezing night, the snow already deep. Wesley had a screwdriver with him; he dug and dug into the ice on the windshield of Candy's car.

This I wasn't told, but it can be inferred: At sunrise, when the sun edged over an iron cloud, the words I LOVE YOU glittered back at it from the furrowed ice.

## 4. *Thin Ice*

A boy fell through the ice today. He must have been playing hooky, alone out there in the bright emptiness. Firemen came to rescue him, but it was too late.

I'm told that, as they were hoisting out his ice-filmed body, it caught a direct ray of sun and shone with all the colors of the rainbow.

## 5. *The Sunset Cat*

To Jo, all weather is great. Whatever she finds when she walks out the door—snow, rain, heat, wind—it's great. She runs, babbles, and whirls with the elation.

To me, these first evenings of spring are like nothing else. Toward sunset the returned birds make a drowsy music so sweet I have to keep it out, protect myself. Jo stops to collect rocks and sticks—toys strewn in fantastic bounty on the ground. A cat comes up to us, asks a bemused question, scampers off.

Fishermen fish in the still evening; old people sit talking on benches under the trees. Across the water the sun is sinking into the woods, a lone, conical flame against deep, shy blue. Jo responds to the flat stretch of grass with hilarity. The two of us are a harmony of contrasts: fast and slow, doing and thinking, loud and quiet; yet somehow in touch, making a whole. People are friendly in this atmosphere: Strangers nod hello, comment and chuckle toward Jo. Not a cloud, not a breeze. The pond is like liquid dusk.

We stay till the fishermen are going home with their catch, a last bird is singing in the darkened maples, and the evening star is out over the woods.

"FAR AWAY, DEEP in the woods, farther than people ever go, there lives a cat, called the sunset cat. The sunset cat sleeps all day and all night, and he only comes out at one time: at sunset. Now when he comes out, he's very beautiful, because his fur glows with all the colors of the sunset—orange and yellow and red and purple—his fur can reflect all the colors from the sun and the clouds. The birds look down from their trees, and they see something that looks like a soft, colorful cloud floating along the floor of the forest. When they see that, they think to themselves—the sunset cat! ... and they all start singing very beautifully.

"The sunset cat comes out at sunset because he has something very important to do. The woods where he lives is where the sun goes every night when it sinks—the sun has a little glass house there where it sleeps. It sleeps there all night while it's dark and the moon's out and the stars are out, and then, when the night's almost over, when it's all rested, it can get up and cross under the earth to the eastern woods, where it rises and makes it day.

"Now when the sun comes sinking into the woods, every night at sunset, it's dangerous. It looks just like a big, bright, orange ball coming down through the trees. Now, if somebody saw it then, and felt like catching it, they could. And if the sun was caught it would be a bad thing. There would be no more day, and it would always be night on the earth. Things wouldn't be able to grow, and it would get very cold, and people would forget what day was like. They'd think that there was never anything except night.

"But the sunset cat stops that from happening. As the sun's coming down into the woods, the sunset cat guards it. He stands under it, reflecting its light and glowing so brightly that if anyone comes near, they have to close their eyes and turn away from the brightness. So if anyone comes who might want to catch the sun, they can't, because the brightness of the sunset cat keeps them away. In that way the sun gets to its glass house and goes to sleep safely every night. And every morning it rises, and crosses under the earth, and makes it day again."

## 6. *Mrs. London's Spring*

A few years ago Mrs. London got permission to grow vegetables behind our building. Every spring she pats, prods, and prunes out there in her little square of earth, engrossed as a novelist lost among his drafts. Sometimes, I guess when it's too hot or when her back's been bothering her, she takes a break and goes down to the pond to fish.

I don't talk with Mrs. London much, but enough to know a little about her. She and her husband moved here five years ago. Two years after that her husband died. That meant the canceling of many plans; if Mrs. London refers to the matter, it's always from this angle of changed plans. Her husband was a factory foreman, she a seamstress. They had no children.

Mrs. London is hefty, her face thick and settled-looking; but give her any slight chance and she turns out to be primed to talk. Her talk is full of tributes to the old days, when people knew about what was around them—plants, animals, other people. It's also, I'm afraid, boring. She sees everyone as equally interested in weather, agriculture, and pond life. You can change the subject, but she waits mildly till you're through, then picks up where she left off.

Still, she's good to have around. Jo was playing outside one day with Pearl, when suddenly Bucky, red, floppy-eared terror of Sun Hill, came over and scooped Pearl up in his mouth. Seeing her baby whisked over to the pond—and dumped in the muck a good five yards out—Jo sat there screaming Pearl's name. But Mrs. London was near. Who else would have waded out—barefoot—and dug through the muck until she struck Pearl? Who else would have taken Pearl as well as Jo (still bawling) inside and washed them both off, then sent them both shiny and cheery into the grass to play again?

When my story gets stuck—every two minutes or so—I lean back in my chair till I can see Mrs. London. There she is, bent bearlike over her vegetables, digging and fussing. Her plans are changed: This isn't the spring she pictured. But still a spring. She keeps tilling the ground.

# 7. Full Circle

The sky was in a bad mood last night. Black clouds came at evening, sealing in the air that was already warm and thick from the day so that everything went still and dead. The full moon came up misty and yellow, with something of evil, of mania in its light.

It didn't take me long, walking out on the balcony at nine, to realize what had happened. Every year about the end of May the weather goes haywire like this, as if spring had finally burst its banks. Already during the day—all day long—the frogs and insects of the pond had been making a crazy, trilling, cooing music—"banter," my wife calls it—that unhinges your mind. And now you stand watching the cracked moon slither in and out of the dark clouds.

It's difficult, when this happens, not to believe in unidentified flying objects. I don't know what else to call them—the green and yellow lights that, on a night like this, go racing around the sky—some form of agitated heat lightning; or maybe they're meteors that couldn't get through the thick air and went into orbit instead. You have an ale, and another, and another; but even they can't shake the grim feeling you get from the blackness and stillness. If you believed in omens, you'd see enough of them tonight to wonder if you should continue in this earthly trek.

AND AFTER MIDNIGHT the dreams came.

My wife dreamed that she and her family were at the lake where they used to stay in the summer; but there was an infestation of some sort of "creatures" in the lake. She approached the shore; she asked her father if it was all right, but he said: "You better not." The water looked calm; but then something started to *rise* from it—

She sat up straight.

Pond music, moonlight ... She climbed out of bed, went to the window. The moon had just started its slow fall; but now, in a clear patch of blue space, it shone from a supreme stillness. She saw the buildings and trees in its light.

Sometime later, apparently, I dreamed I was a passenger in a small plane that was supposed to land along a coast. Preparing to land, the plane swung out in an arc over the sea—and kept swinging, farther and farther out—

Now I sat up straight; and sat that way awhile in the banter-filled darkness.

My mother, a few miles from us, was dreaming about the war. People were crawling in a neat file through a long underground tunnel; but whether they were crawling to or from the enemy was uncertain. That was all I gathered about that one.

It CLEARED SOMEWHAT toward morning. A breeze blew some of the clouds away, roused the air from its stuffy sleep. The birds made a calmer music; by the time we woke up there was sunlight on the curtains and they were still singing. Jo was already moving around singing to herself in her room. We ate breakfast bleary-eyed, sipping coffee as if doing a delicate experiment; I skimmed some news. Afterward, figuring out that it was the last weekend of May and it would probably be open, we gathered our things and left for the pool.

# Two More Tries at It

I KNOW AN ASTRONOMER. Once there were only about a dozen people in the world who understood the intricacies of his work; but he kept turning further and further into himself, his own investigations, and now there are even fewer, if any.

When he interviewed me about becoming his editor, I explained that, for my part, I have no comprehension whatsoever of his work. But he said that was all right, as long as I could help with the English. In all the time since he hired me, though, he hasn't written a single thing. Yet I've still had to spend many hours in his study—he says my presence helps his concentration, and he wants me to be on hand in case anything does happen.

There's very little room to sit safely in his study. I'm usually hunched up in a chair in one corner, he at his desk by the window. The rest of the floor is taken up by a peculiar setup, a sort of miniature solar system that he made: Round a big sunlike globe on a stand in the middle revolve smaller globes that seem to correspond, more or less, to our solar system. At least there's a little, outer, greenish one that I associate with Pluto, a much larger one with not exactly rings but a faint silver aura that I think of as Saturn. On the other hand, there seem to be a lot more of them—it's hard to count exactly—than in our solar system. And there are a couple—one that's just a blur of daubed colors, almost like a floating rainbow; another that's very strange, not round but sort of cone-shaped, and seems, when it comes near me, to be making a low humming sound—that I can't identify at all.

At any rate, I always have to stay alert, because sometimes one of them flies right at my head and I have to duck. They make quite a racket knocking against the walls; I gather that his wife, whom I sometimes hear clanging pots downstairs, is none too happy with the whole business. He sits motionless by the window, watching his experiment; behind his head a real planet, maybe large, gold Jupiter, starts to glow in the bluish dusk. I feel guilty about getting good pay essentially to do nothing, doubtful about this project of his, and concerned that—well, that all the components of his mind might not be holding together. And yet I can't help getting the feeling, as the night deepens and the room grows dark, with only the sun-globe glowing in the center, the busy little balls flying and knocking—his head a grave silhouette with stars behind it—I can't help at least suspecting that some sort of very serious research is indeed going on here.

# 2

I know a mystic. He wants me to interpret dreams for him. I told him I know absolutely nothing about interpreting dreams. He said that's all right, I'm an editor, I can put them into writing.

He has me sleep outside on his balcony with him. The idea is that, if he wakes up with a dream, he'll be able to wake me up too, and I'll be right there to "interpret"—write it down, in good English—for him. He says he dreams deeper and purer dreams when he sleeps outside.

This has been going on for a few months; but still he's never woken me up to tell me anything. He says to be patient; these things take time. Mystics, I guess, have to sink very deeply into their minds before they can dig anything out of them.

Meanwhile, there's something to be said for sleeping out on a balcony several nights a week. I usually lie awake a lot longer—he falls asleep quickly—than he; I like to see the stars, feel the breezes that drift across my face and rustle the leaves all down the street.

Not long ago there was a particularly beautiful night with a full moon. The light flooded us on the balcony; the chairs and flowerpots were there almost as if it was daytime. It didn't seem to affect him—he's a strange guy, doesn't say much, very routinized in his behavior; soon he was snoring away. But I lay awake a long time, looking up at the sky.

I must have fallen asleep and dreamed, because it seemed to me that the moon had come very near the earth—so near, in fact, that I'd somehow left the balcony and was walking on its surface. I was ankle-deep in a sea of fog; around me bright-colored planets came floating into view—I thought I could make out red Mars, a large, lonely, bluish Uranus with its little flock of moons. I was in ecstasy.

When I woke up, the fog was still there—it was dawn on the balcony. A strange idea was in my mind: I wanted to tell *him* about the dream so that *he* could put it in some kind of shape before *I* forgot it. But as I scrambled up from my sleeping bag, I found that in all the fog I couldn't make him out; and I must have crawled back into my sleeping bag and forgotten about it.

By now, of course, I'm not even sure that the part with the dawn mist on the balcony wasn't also part of the dream. Or at least, I'm led to think that way by another strange thing that happened.

Just a few mornings later, when I woke up, he was sitting, with a sullen, annoyed look, on the parapet staring out at the street. He told me that during the night he'd at last had a dream—something he couldn't remember clearly anymore, about being in a rowboat in an ocean—but when he tried to wake me up, I lay like a log and the most he could get out of me was a mutter or two. Wasn't this what he'd hired me for? I was very sorry, and told him so.

Now the peculiar thing was that, as I sat and thought about it, I too began to remember things about the night that had passed. It seemed—I don't know how else to explain it—that I had been with him in the dream about the rowboat; only, if anything, I found myself able to recall it more vividly than he. A northern sea … ice floating in the water, brilliant red clouds … Yes, I'd been—by now I was hunched in one corner of the balcony, my head deep in my hands—I'd been there in the boat, sitting across from him, our faces shimmering red!

And—yes—he'd handed me something ... a pen! ... and I'd ... *written something*!! ... I darted over to the notebook beside my sleeping bag, snatched it up and flapped through it excitedly—and, of course, there was nothing but blank pages.

By this time he was looking at me oddly. I turned to him eagerly, notebook in hand; but when I tried to explain, such a jumble of words rushed up in me that ... I just said nothing and looked at him.

Unhappy as he was about my not waking up, he didn't dismiss me. Another full moon is coming; I know he regards the dream about the rowboat as just a preliminary, a prelude. We keep sleeping out, two dark shapes on our balcony. Around us is the night, listening and waiting.

# Blind Dating in Jerusalem

A KIND OF BLIND date I don't recommend is where one participant is already a veteran of the blind-dating scene, the other a novice. The former is disillusioned and has lowered his standards; he's prepared to accept anything that seems reasonably appealing, even if he doesn't feel that a grand concourse of souls has taken place. The latter still has very high standards, and feels that she has time on her hands; the dating agency, she's certain, will send her one intriguing candidate after another—until, by the fifteenth one, the twentieth, the thirtieth, she at last strikes gold, something close to her inner image of perfection.

They find a pleasant retreat in the bar-restaurant of a hotel; the waitress brings him his Amstel, her her tea, almost demonstratively leaves them to their undisturbed quietude. I thought, at first, that living alone would be difficult; actually it's kind of pleasant, with all that time that I can decide to spend as I want … Well, I don't have that issue. Since he left, the minute I get home the girls want all of my attention, all the time. It wears me down. Maybe they'll get more used to it … I'm sorry to hear that. Yes, it may just be too big a change for them at this point … He thinks: Her face is pretty, and though, in her thick winter clothes, one can't make out much else, she's neither overly fat nor overly thin. She seems a decent sort—clearly no thief, embezzler, blackmailer. She, for her part, thinks: No, that's not it.

The evening draws on toward its climax—Well, I'd be glad to meet again. A winter night in Jerusalem; outside, squalls of rain hurl themselves at buildings, stray cats scamper. The beer glass, tea mug, long empty; the paraffin lamp burns sedately on the table. She sits back ... I'm not sure. No? he queries. I'm not sure if it flows—if there's much sympathy between us. He inspects the check the waitress has left; digs out his credit card, as well as a generous tip.

## 2

Tourism to Jerusalem has waned. In every hotel, many rooms stand empty. They're filled, by day, with nothing but light and silence; by night—with nothing. A cleaning lady may come in and whisk her way through. If the empty rooms are on high floors—and most of them are, since most of the vacationers who do come don't want to be bothered with long elevator rides—then they're neighbors of the sky, almost part of it.

Many of the hotels lay off their pianists, or continue not to employ any. In bars, in coffeehouses, in carpeted lounges next to windows, pianos stand, unused. They have a silent eloquence; their keys are ready, their form is perfect. White pianos, beige ones, black ones. Islands of silence—but beyond silence, since of all the things in the hotels they have the greatest capacity to speak.

Unemployed pianists lie in empty rooms. They count the minutes, the hours of the day, while the sky changes and the clouds pass. They've stopped calling the hotels to ask if there's an opening for work. Their ability to play the piano stands, within them, silent and eloquent as the pianos stand in the hotels. The sky drifts over their roofs.

## 3

At night, when we dream, we have blind dates with strange beings and entities—our parents, our memories, God, scraps of music. I once, in a dream, had a chance meeting with God. He was sitting in a train station, a small, hunched man in a long grey coat, a wide-brimmed hat that covered most of his face, a wispy white beard emerging beneath the hat. None of the other people who were waiting seemed aware of him; but I sensed, suddenly, who he was with a deep awe and dread. I felt that I should say something to him; but I also realized that I wasn't prepared for this meeting. I didn't know him, or what sort of thing one should say to him; and I didn't think he knew me.

When I was younger, I thought I'd always be young, but all the time they were arranging for me a blind date with getting older. Now that it's really happening, I don't know what to make of it; just observe sometimes that it really is happening. What if I were to meet it at some restaurant, sit across a table from it, try to make conversation? Would we hit it off, get to know each other better?

Every year I have a blind date with spring. By now, of course, I've seen a few dozen springs, and it shouldn't be so unfamiliar. Yet every year it comes almost like a total stranger, about whom I know very little. It starts with waking up one morning a little earlier than usual, a different sort of light in the room. The sound of outside is different—a soft void, a calm emptiness. Opening the blinds, I see that a gentle vagueness is over everything, almost as if the sea had flowed inland, immersed the trees and buildings. When I leave my flat to walk to work, the sun is up and it's still like that—wading through a sea; clouds of soft green leaves, watery gleams. The blackbirds sing, the almond blossoms shine. I don't know what it is. I've never seen it before.

I have a blind date with blindness. To find out, at this age, that I know nothing, don't know what anything is. I see things, and it's as if I've never seen them before. What is spring? What is Jerusalem? I sit across a table from my blindness, and the conversation doesn't flow, we don't know each other.

# I'll See You There

As usual on Monday nights, business was slow, and there weren't many dishes coming in for Lenny to wash. He sat perched on a balanced dish rack in front of the big dishwashing machine; it was seven-thirty now, and if it stayed slow like this they might let him leave by eight.

Across the long kitchen the cook was pacing from pot to pot, checking and stirring, puckering up his face as steam shot out into it.

"Busy over there, son?" he called.

Lenny turned toward him.

"Got any pots?"

The cook glanced behind him at the sink. "Couple. You could do 'em if you want."

Lenny didn't answer him; he leaned back into the machine. He sighed and rubbed his eyes. Tired. Which was good—maybe he'd be able to sleep tonight. That was the nice thing about this job—since he'd gotten it he'd been sleeping better. Sometimes, when he woke up in the morning for school, he didn't feel quite as horrible.

He opened his eyes; waited for them to focus; saw Jane, the head waitress, a hefty woman about fifty with a platinum hairdo sort of like a turban, unloading glasses from a tray beside him.

"Tired there, Lenny?"

"Yeah." He stood up and started putting the glasses into a dish rack.

"The jerk out there might give you a break tonight."

"Hope so." He turned and saw her looking at him queerly.

"Don't you ever smile?"

He grinned. "Rarely."

"How long've you been here now? I don't think I've seen you smile once. What about you, Roy? You ever seen him smile?"

"Not lately."

"What is it? Don't like this place?"

Lenny stood leaning back against the machine. "It's not the greatest place, I guess."

"No. That's for sure. But I've been workin' here six years now under the jerk, and if I didn't joke around with the customers and the other girls, I'd have flipped a long time ago. Laughin' is what helps you. You gotta do it. Even when you don't feel like it."

"Shoulda been a preacher, Jane," called the cook.

"Yeah, but not for the likes of you."

She looked, worried, at Lenny.

"What do you do when you're not workin' in this pit?"

"Uh ... read quite a lot."

Lenny saw the manager, a stocky man with black hair and a bulldog face, enter through the doorway behind her.

"Read? Well, that's something. You need something like that to relax. Me, when I'm not in this hole I play canasta a lot. It just helps you AOW!"—she shrieked as one hand shot to her rump. The manager, who had pinched her, stood there grinning.

"Vincent! You got problems or something? What's the matter, you horny in your pants tonight?"

The manager chuckled. "Come on. Pahty waitin' out theah."

"Don't worry, don't worry, you horny son-of-a-gun." She hurried past him out the door. The manager looked at Lenny.

"What have you bin doin'?"

Lenny was still leaning back against the dishwasher. "Uh, nothing, I was just—"

"Well get the hell over on those pots theah, fuh Christ's sake! Shit, you don't wanna do the work, I can get somebody else easy. People like you I can get a dime a dozen. Damn shit. You pay people now so they can come in and sit on their ass. Think they can come in here and blab with the waitresses all night. Don't need any of that shit. Shit, I ain't Santa Claus."

Lenny, over at the sink, turned on the soap faucet and watched blankly as the soap began pouring into the wrong basin, the rinsing basin; then he slapped the faucet over to the other side. The foam began to collect and steam began to rise, meaning the soap was too hot. He flicked the cold dial and the soap, of course, was soon too cold.

"Aa, shit."

"Got caught this time, huh?" the cook said behind him.

Lenny said nothing.

The cook made a little grunt, started whistling.

Lenny took a big pot covered with dried tomato-sauce stains, shoved it down into the soap, began scrubbing fiercely with a rag that seemed too flimsy for the task.

# 2

Sometime later, when he was about halfway through the pots, he heard a voice behind him. He turned and saw the manager, standing by a soda keg.

"Take this over to the bah, will you."

Lenny let the rag fall into the water, dried his hands on his apron, took the heavy keg from the manager. "When you come back and finish duh pots, you can go."

The bar was dimly lit, a slower place than the kitchen. Slow-moving people sat over drinks; a crowd roared in a television set.

The bartender looked at him, said: "Bring that right over here why don't you son."

Lenny stepped behind the bar, aware of eyes that didn't really see him; he set the keg down at the bartender's feet.

"Thanks son."

"Yup."

On his way out of the bar, someone standing by the coat rack said something to him. He stopped and looked. It was a girl, with a thin, bright face framed by long, thick, reddish-brown hair. She was look-ing at him.

"Pardon me?" Lenny said.

"I said Hi."

"Oh. Hi."

"Is your name Larry?"

"Lenny. Can I help you?"

"Do you wait on table here?"

Her voice was low, hard to hear; her green eyes kept looking at him. She was around his age, but not from his school; he didn't think he'd ever seen her before.

"Nah, I just wash dishes."

"That must keep you busy."

"Yeah, it does."

She kept looking at him, not saying anything.

He said: "You from around here?"

"Nope."

"Where you from?"

"I'm from south of here."

"South of here?"

"Yup."

"Listen, I have to get back to washing these pots, or this manager's going to execute me."

"What time do you leave?"

"*Leave?*"

"Yeah, leave. Here. Tonight."

She still kept looking at him—as if she could see very deep inside him and saw things that amused her.

He said: "Pretty soon, actually. Eight-thirty I'd say."

"What door do you leave by?"

"What?"

"What door you go out by?"

"Oh, uh, back door, right over that way, past the kitchen."

"You have a car?"

"Yeah. Blue Rambler. It's way over by the fence."

"So I'll see you there."

"By the car?"

"Yeah."

"All right. All right."

"I'll see you there Larry. *Lenny.*"

"OK."

He stared; she gave him a final, bright look and walked away.

HE WALKED BACK into the kitchen in a daze. He saw Jane, writing a check, and Roy, stirring. He went back to the sink and the pots and stood there, unsure what to do. Water. Wash. Pot. He flicked the faucet on, fished out the rag from the brown water. Oh my God, he thought, starting to scrub, oh hell ... "Larry": It was funny. Someone else had once told him he looked like a Larry. Who, though?—Danny Slocum? ... he stopped; what the hell was he doing? He wiped his forehead, grabbed a pot and plunged it into the rinsing basin. Who the hell was she...? What did it matter? He could take her somewhere in the car. He'd had *some* experience. Three times—but who were they? He tried to remember who were the three he'd had experience with.

He stood flustered, one hand holding the rag and the other dipped halfway into the water.

A SHARP WIND stirred the snow up from the asphalt and blew it in mad circles and swoops. Just past the parking lot stood the black, stark forms of trees. He sat on the trunk of his car, shivering, hands clenched in his pockets, swinging his legs back and forth. It hadn't been so long yet. Jane had left only ten minutes ago—he'd seen her trudging to her car in her scarf and long coat. That meant it was only a little after ten o'clock—the bar was still open, would be for a long time. Above him stars gleamed in the blue-black sky.

# Sid's Blues

THEY BURIED ME thirty feet deep in a meadow outside of
town. The reason? Based on the record, there were sufficient
grounds to suspect me of vampire inclinations. Not only did I
have vampire forebears, but as a kid I'd been unwise enough to report
some troubling, violent dreams to my parents, who, in turn, had been
unwise enough to report the issue to a shrink, to whom they'd forced
me to go for a while.

I should explain that the vampire curse is quite common in
Minnesota. In most communities, though, it doesn't pose a problem: Vampire-suspects are just cremated when they die. Only a few
old-fashioned communities like Kescogee still cling to the outmoded
practice of deep burial. Deep burial is more respectful of the natural cycle and all that, but the trouble is that it doesn't work—at least
not more than about two-thirds of the time. It may seem incredible,
but the other third or so of deep-buried vampires do rise up. It happened several times while I was alive, sometimes with dire results.
Everybody knows this; but nobody—or at least not the majority of the
voters—does anything about it.

Myself, I wish they would—just for the vampires' sake if nothing
else. Waking up in a coffin is the worst part. It's also no joy to claw
your way up through thirty feet of rock, clay, and sand to the surface.
Vampires, because they're stronger than live people and have less need
for food or oxygen, can do this, but it's not an enviable experience.

And then, risen again, you confront the future. You're a pariah
now. The best you can hope for, if you don't want to spend the next

two or three years roaming the fields and eating berries, is to succeed as an impostor among the living. But the chances of succeeding at it aren't good: Every cop has your mug shot memorized, and you'll have to steer very clear of people who used to know you. If caught, you get executed and quickly cremated; not even the pious want to give vampires a second chance.

And let's say this doesn't happen—that you don't get caught; that you do manage to pass yourself off in some miserable parody of a human life. There's not much to look forward to; risen vampires never live longer than two or three years, and the death is sudden and none too pleasant. Your friends, if they're around, can't offer much sympathy; they're too shocked that you were a vampire all this time. This might be called the circuitous path to cremation.

Could be worse. Among other distractions, I have the challenge of trying to piece together what happened. As I see it now, it would have been exactly a week ago, Friday, that the fatal mishap occurred. Friday, because I seem to remember considering stopping at Moe's Pub after getting out of work later that afternoon—something I generally did on that day to honor, drown, another ludicrous week. But I didn't make it that far. I guess it was when I was walking back from my lunch break that the thing happened, something with a vehicle reeling around the corner at me as I stepped into the road. I deduce that it was three days later that I was buried; and it would have been the next day, Tuesday, that I rose up.

Since then I've mostly been wandering around Kescogee; last night, instead of the park, I slept in a flophouse. Yes, I've committed a crime, not too horrifying I think: Yesterday I mugged this well-appointed guy on a sidewalk. I just made a fake gun under my ratty jacket and requested his wallet. I lucked out—a handy sum. The problem was that I had to buy clothes. The suit they'd buried me in was no longer in the best shape, not what you'd call presentable. It was fine for roaming like a bum, but not for anything more ambitious than that. Anyway, my colleagues at the flophouse got a kick out of it when I changed into my new, nicer garments; one of them actually asked if I'd dug the other getup out of some casket.

That leaves only a few bucks; but for now I'm happy just to look passable. Tonight, strange to say, I have a party to go to.

I SAID BEFORE that vampires have to keep away from anyone they used to know in life. So it might seem surprising that I'm on my way to a party at the *Chrysalis* office where I used to work. The *Chrysalis* staff, though, aren't ordinary folk. If someone breaks into an old man's home, knocks him down, and steals his money, they're likely to blame it on the old man—he was probably, after all, of higher social status than the other guy. They wouldn't be likely to report someone—even a risen vampire—to the authorities. Claire, the secretary, would be the only one to worry about; but in the *Chrysalis* setting I expect she, too, will be OK.

*Chrysalis* is a small counterculture monthly. I was its copyeditor for about ten years—my last ten years, as it turned out, of more or less normal life. I had nothing to get me through this world but a flair for English, so that was the niche I found. The last half-year at *Chrysalis* I'd been in love with a new graphics editor, Ellen Duane. A going-away party for Bill Harstad, who'd gotten an offer from another magazine in Chicago, was supposed to be today after work. I was greatly looking forward to it—a chance to be drunk and act silly around her—and, even now, I figure I might as well stop by.

I say "in love" mainly to give myself a little thrill. I've never been in love and wouldn't know what it feels like. If, though, there was ever anyone who gave my heart some flutters, it was Ellen. It wasn't a matter of being taken with her. I could see her weaknesses the first time I met her—shy, apologetic, chronically without belief in herself, keyed-up to prove her abilities in the job; and I could see, too, the simple way to get on her good side: be nice to her. She was pushing thirty, with a pleasant build, a round, endearing face, dejectedly honest eyes. She just wanted someone to be nice to her; I would have liked to be the one.

Not that my infatuation was any secret to her. I was used to living off the scraps flirtation throws to the needy, master of the awkward glance, the suggestive phrase. There was a time, maybe her first two months at *Chrysalis*, when she'd always show up at my cubicle to ask about this or that; she was shyly waiting for me to make some approach. Then a phase of dull confusion as the expectation faded; finally a leveling-off into a kind of muted, wistful affection between us. I knew I couldn't go after Ellen. With her it would have had to be serious; and my secret flaw ran too deep.

*Chrysalis* inhabits the top two stories of an old building on D'Arcy Street two blocks off Main in downtown Kescogee. Walking down D'Arcy Street, I have the same feeling I used to have back then: What's the point? Random people in sullen buildings, eking out lives with no apparent purpose. After a clear day the air is in its bluish hush before night. I don't feel nostalgia exactly—more like: This is the world, this is D'Arcy Street, after I'm gone. Sadness that it hasn't changed—that it wasn't my presence, after all, that spoiled it, but something from its own endless past that will go on endlessly into its future.

It's hard to tell, listening to them, how much they're letting the sudden death of a coworker last week subdue the mood of their party. I could think that there's a chastened quality to their chatter, but it could just be a muffled intensity. True, Harstad was leaving, and they had to have a sendoff party. Maybe, though, their finding out who I really was—or potentially was—has dampened their grief.

I stand in the dim stairwell one floor below them. Around the bend is the third floor—empty and still now—where I used to work.

Going up the last, slowest flight, I can hear their particular voices— the garrulous grumble of Hogan, Sternczak's question-statements, Claire and Debby's titter and chitter. Nothing of Ellen. I stop—a step or two into the hall—to comb my hair, straighten my shirt. Vampires, I should explain, are somewhat different from what they were in life. I'm bigger, my voice lower, my eyes uncontrollably reddish. I could use another shave, too; that one this morning at the hotel wasn't enough. But otherwise I look decent, I think—as far as I'm concerned, the same Sid Gonyoe. True, none of them knew about my problem back then; the only ones who did were my parents of blessed memory, my brother Bud, and the police department. But by now, of course, they all do. So, are they really so liberal?—here's the test.

The hall opens out to the left into a big room they call the conference room. From my shadow now I can just see the bearded silhouette of Schiller, the editor in chief, straddling a backwards chair and discoursing to someone across the table. They still have the lights out; there's just the dusk light from the window. Mishap or no, they sound pretty merry. Well, that was my philosophy, too—don't let death spoil what little there is of life.

I go and stand in the opening. Judy Thomson stops next to me with a wineglass in her hand. "Hi, Sid."

"Hi."

It's a combination of her turning and saying "Sid's here, everyone" and their having noticed it anyway. Only Sternczak keeps asking-stating and Roice chuckling-agreeing by the window. Also by the window, alone, is Ellen.

"Sid!" Schiller says loudly.

"How you doing."

Now Sternczak stops—then Roice.

Schiller still straddles his chair—glass held very still. "Didn't know you'd be joining us."

I can see most of their faces—not Ellen's—a shape by the window—against blue dusk.

"You uh … rose up, I take it," says Schiller.

"If you want to put it that way."

"Sid wouldn't put it that way," says Harstad.

"He'd edit that right out," says Sternczak.

I smile. "Same old Sid."

That throws them a moment.

"I get you something, Sid?" Claire says—standing up, too fast.

"Sure."

## 2

Talking with them, I find out that in my current state I'm much more in touch with undercurrents than I was in life. I can know directly what before I only sensed, half-knew, or evaded. With Schiller, for instance, I was never comfortable—not even when seemingly most free and cordial with him; he wasn't only the boss but also had something fundamentally sardonic about him, something that made you feel you were an irredeemable failure. Between Judy and me, on the other hand, there's a mutual, melancholy, mystified liking, made distant by her being too tidy and straightforward. Roice has sort of an attraction to me—I could dismiss it, it's OK, but it makes him too uneasy. Harstad and I come from crossed stars—different ways of talking, thinking, being; any exchange between us is a clash of swords, and anything said can at best be taken as a feint. To Claire I gave sort of a housemother role at *Chrysalis*. She wasn't entirely happy with this—she has breasts and a rear end like the younger women, didn't like this sexless designation; and the puzzling and disappointing tension between us came from this tussle of my appointing her and her declining to be this maternal figure.

After their first shock, they're taking it better. They're people who like to feel that they *know*, that all of reality is under their purview. Already now they're assimilating me into what they think they know: Yes, this is Sid, just Sid, a victim of the archaic and senseless practice of deep burial, therefore a member of the grand class of the Victimized, therefore benign and a friend of theirs. Not that they show any interest in what I've been through in the last few days—you'd think, for instance, that people would be curious about what it's like to wake up in a coffin. Instead, they all use a certain ritual that consists of saying my name and drawing me into *their* conversation: "Sid, we got a piece from Arnold Sindermann this week"; "So Governor Busbee vetoed the restitution bill again. I don't know, Sid."

I stay mostly near the table, where the food is—and especially the drink. The gin and tonics don't seem to affect my mind, but I have to dissemble my manic craving for the taste. Ellen stood at the border of some of my conversations, but now she's over by the window again talking with Trish Irwin. Where she goes, I follow—not just my gaze, but *I*. She's my link to … no good words for it. *Shantih*. In life, too, she was this link; now, in death, it's too late to pretend it doesn't matter.

I FINALLY FIND myself standing with her by the window. Dark outside—stars over the town—and almost dark, except broken light from the hall, in the conference room.

I stand so close to her our clothes are almost touching.

"So how've you been?"

"OK. A little upset."

"About what?"

"About Sid's accident."

"Well … Could have been worse."

"Did you—when did you rise up?"

"Tuesday."

"So … what were you doing?"

"Nothing. Roaming around."

"Glad you seem … intact."

"It's not so bad being like this. In some ways it's better."

"That's surprising."

"Well, you know more about yourself … like what you really care about."

My hand goes to her arm.

She's quiet for a long time. I sip my drink. She has on the blue dress, the one I like that makes her slight and slim.

"Lots of surprises," she finally says.

"What's a surprise?"

"This."

"Was it a secret?"

"Almost."

"I can't believe that."

"Almost."

My hand moves on her arm.

I say: "Can we go someplace?"

Leaving, I feel their gazes on us; I know they're uneasy. But I also hear their rationalizations clicking away like keyboards.

HER CAR IS a couple of blocks down D'Arcy. For some reason, I go and stand at the driver's side; she comes over to the door and I say:

"Oh, sorry"; but she silently gestures and goes around herself to the passenger's side.

I roll down the window and feel the cool air wash over me. It may be the gin and tonics affecting me more than I know, or maybe just my enhanced senses, but that's how the air feels—like cool water.

"I was wondering," I say—Ellen has also gotten in, "if you'd live with me."

She waits. "On the first date?"

"Something wrong with that?"

"No."

"Wouldn't have to be in Kescogee. We could go somewhere … get new papers … get a new name for me. People do it all the time."

"What about *Chrysalis*?"

"Oh. Well. I'll work. You can too. You can look for something good."

"You rose up three days ago."

"So?"

"You just started in this … changed situation. I don't see how you could be so sure of yourself."

I grin twistedly. "I can be sure about a lot of things. *You* seem to be the one who's not sure."

"It's a lot all at once."

We sit awhile in the coolness.

I say, "It could be a good three years."

"What could?"

"What?"

"I don't know what you're saying, three years."

"That's how long a vampire lives. At the most."

"I knew that."

"All too well."

"What? What did you say?"

People go by—footsteps, talking—then silent again.

I say: "It would be hard living with someone in my status. I realize that. I might get picked up. Even if I don't, in three years I croak—and where does that leave you. All I can say is—those years would be like nothing else you'll ever experience, before or after. Three years of … perfection. Perfect love."

"I believe that."

"Well then what's the trouble."

"There's no trouble. This is just very sudden and … we don't know each other all that well."

I rub my forehead. "I can tell you this: We know all we need to know about each other."

"Maybe."

I sit glumly.

Finally I say: "Can I kiss you at least?"

"Yes."

I have to go all the way across the seat to her—she just waits. A decent kiss—but now I feel something else, deep inside, rising up.

# 3

My older brother Bud lives alone in an old farmhouse near the North Dakota border. He makes a living repairing TVs and radios and just about anything else people want to bring him. I never liked him. He's gruff and moody, won't really let you get close to him.

His house is a good two hundred yards off the road. Still dark out as I drive down the long driveway. My windows are wide open, and I can hear the birds awakening; seems cold for July. Stars way out over the fields.

Even though I've had my lights out, it's a relief to shut off the motor. I sit there a minute hearing the birds. His house is pitch-dark; it's just like him not to leave a single light on, but I know he has a shotgun to keep him safe. Wonder how I'll work this. Wouldn't want him to shoot me.

Getting out, I close the door soft as I can but flinch anyway at the noise. Colder, clearer, sweeter-smelling, louder out here. I plod silently across the smooth driveway to the lawn. The dew soaks right up through my flimsy canvas shoes. Next to his door there's a steel mailbox he made—can just see the black lettering: GONYOE. Always struck me as strange that he, too, called himself that.

I rap once, twice, with the metal knocker.

I start to do it again—and then hear him in there.

Right at this point I change my mind: should never have come here; should have kept due north without stopping.

"Who's there?"

His voice—right behind the door.

"Sid"—doesn't come out well.

"Who's there?"

"Sid."

"*What.*"

"Sid. Your brother."

"My brother's dead."

"I'm here, Bud. I came back."

A light goes on overhead. The doorknob turns this way, that way, clicks.

Bud stands haggard in his robe, grimacing in the glare, pointing a shotgun toward me. When he makes me out—I don't look my best— he steps back, despite the shotgun.

"Sid—is that you?"

"It's all right, Bud. You can stop pointing that at me. It's all right."

He doesn't. "What do you want?"

"To ask you something."

He peers out over my shoulder. "That your car out there?"

"Y—no. Yeah."

He moves his peering gaze to me. "What?"

"Yeah. It's my car."

"Why … what are you doing here?" The gun goes down, finally.

"Drove. From Kescogee."

"Tonight?"

"Yeah."

"What for?"

"Something I needed to ask you."

THAT LEGEND, THAT vampires can't see themselves in the mirror, isn't true unfortunately. In the bathroom I catch a glimpse; none too charming.

Bud's waiting for me in the kitchen, perched on the counter. Behind him, a window open on the cool night. He's been nice enough, I notice as I slump down in a chair at the table, to put the gun where I can't see it, but I'm sure it's nearby somewhere.

I sit rubbing my eyes—not trying to control the sound of my hoarse breathing.

Bud says: "I get you something?"

I blink at him, waiting for my eyes to focus. "You wouldn't happen to have gin and tonic."

"Gin and tonic?"

I nod.

"Yeah, I've got gin and tonic. That's what you want?"

"If you can … if it's all right."

Bud looks strange puttering around the counter, squat and square in his robe, sullenly efficient—sort of the way, except the rumpled hair, that dad used to look taking his late ham and cheese sandwich at night. The few times I've seen Bud these last few years, I've noticed him getting more and more like dad—as if, now that dad's gone, he no longer has to pretend he doesn't share the same gruff, standoffish soul. Dad planned for Bud to become an attorney like him; Bud became an appliance repairman. Our home was essentially the site of this drama between them. Mom and I were just skinny, quiet, inconsequential, expected to keep to the side and busy ourselves … History. Birds singing outside.

A fizzing gin and tonic before me.

I sip with great fervor; sit back sharply, sighing.

"So … what happened? You crawled out?" he says, getting back up on the counter.

I nod.

"That priest … he was counting on you to stay down there. In peace."

"Well … easy for him to say."

"When was it—when did you crawl out?"

"Tuesday."

He frowns. "Assumed it was tonight."

I shake my head.

"So you've been—what have you been doing?"

"Hanging around Kescogee."

We both stop, as if "Kescogee" means something too profound to talk about.

Bud moves and says: "Something you were going to ask me?"

"Ask you. Yeah. About the waterfall."

"Petosquit Falls?"

"Yeah."

"What about it?"

"Where is it?"

"From here?"

"Yeah."

"Easy. Go back out on 32, go about two miles till you come to the lumberyard outside of town, go left at the light."

"How far from there?"

"Five minutes. Less. Why? Why do you want to know?"

"Uh … doesn't matter."

"Tell me anyway."

"Well … have to throw someone over it."

He sits very still. "Who?"

"Someone."

"Yourself?"

"No."

"Not yourself."

"No."

"Who?"

"This woman."

"What woman?"

"She's uh … out in the car."

He gazes toward the wall. "That car that's out there?"

"Yeah."

"That's not your car."

"No."

"Whose is it?"

"This woman's."

"She's in there?"

"Yeah."

"She's … "

"Dead."

Bud waits. Behind him, the dawn sounds peaceful to me.

"You killed her?"

"Yeah."

"When?"

"Tonight—last night."

"Why?"

"No reason."

"Anyone you knew?"

"Yeah. Worked with her at *Chrysalis*."

"That's the magazine."

"Yeah."

"What'd you do, break into her place?"

"No. I uh … went to an office party and … we left together."

"Wait a minute. People saw you with her."

"Yeah. They're uh … progressives. They won't … notify anyone."

He doesn't answer, and I say: "She lived alone. Nobody even knows about it yet."

"What are you planning to do?"

"Go to Canada."

"After you throw her over the falls."

"Yeah."

"In a stolen car?"

"Well. I can get rid of that, too."

He stares at me.

He says: "I'm practically an accomplice now."

"Not exactly."

"Just about. Knowing about it, for one thing. Harboring you here, for another. Worse yet—helping you get to the falls."

He keeps staring at me. I won't stare back.

I say: "Back out on 32. Left at the lumberyard."

"You better get a move on." He turns and peers out the window. "Starting to get light."

Glancing at his back, I consider killing him, since he'll probably tell the cops. What the hell for?

"Picked a good waterfall," he says, looking at me again.

"Yeah?"

"Petosquit goes fast. Empties into Crane Lake just over the border."

"Will she get that far?"

"She'll have the rapids to propel her. Stands a good chance."

Now I stare—but not at him or anything—can't speak.

I feel myself pushing back the chair—standing—turning to face him.

He says—lowering himself from the counter: "Don't hurt anyone else, Sid."

"No."

"I feel like … you're making me part of it if you do that."

"No—I'll uh … keep to myself. I plan to."

After a while, I say: "I feel really sorry. I know mom and dad wouldn't have wanted it."

He says—also after a while: "No. I guess they wouldn't have."

A curt, painful handshake.


IT'S SO FOGGY out I can barely see the turnoff where the falls are. Getting out of the car, I can hear the roar, but before me there's just the rocky ground and a huge wall of fog.

Ellen doesn't want to come out. Too bad it couldn't be a four-door. I try balancing her supine—she's very stiff—on the backrest and slowly maneuvering her out, but she keeps sliding off. I try just sort of dragging her over the backrest, but grow fearful of hurting her. Finally, I think to open the hatch.

Carrying her, I set her down, not because she's heavy, but because I've noticed a brooch on her dress—still wearing it. I sit down beside her and spend a while crying.

I smooth some hair back behind her ears; take her hands and pull till they're folded on her dress; leave her like that for someone to find her.

I walk out on a big, flat, glossy-wet rock that juts from the ledge. I go out on it as far as I can; I put out a hand and feel nothing. The falls are to my right; I can taste cool droplets. I look around me—an island in the fog. Shantih.

# The Tundra Cat

THE TUNDRA CAT is a wild cat, only a little bigger than a house cat, which apparently has lived around here as long as anyone knows since it appears in the earliest Inuit myths. I would not say the tundra cat was the only reason I took up the habit of sitting outside in our front garden in the very early morning; but I also wouldn't say it had nothing to do with it.

Our front garden is small and surrounded by a stone wall, with no growing stuff to speak of other than weak grass and a few evergreen shrubs along that wall. I guess it was in August that I started to come out here before dawn, to sit in my parka and shiver—it's always cold here at night, even in summer—while the dark was slowly invaded by a pensive, ambivalent light. How did we end up living in a tiny cottage—not even in a settlement but at some distance from one, a castoff of a castoff—in the grey rock country south of the ice plateau in Greenland? It was puzzling enough to warrant taking some time, in the most still and solitary hour of the day, to sit and wonder about it.

By September the ground of the little garden had already frozen, and I was wearing two and three and four sweaters under my parka but still shivering. It was at dawn, the ground and garden wall lined by a pallid blue ice, that the thing I had been secretly—even, I guess, to myself—waiting for, that maybe had been the true motive for my sitting outside, happened: There appeared on the wall, so out-of-nowhere that it was beyond sudden, all-white and apparition-like, a beautiful and silent tundra cat.

# 2

October. It's good and cold—I keep knocking my mittens together, getting up to stomp around every few minutes. Even though it's before dawn, it's actually about seven in the morning—here, on the chilly side of the Arctic Circle, the days are already getting very short.

I've put little slabs of seal meat at various places on the wall. We don't, of course, eat seal meat; but my wife refuses to let me use regular meat for this purpose, so I had to pick up some cheap seal meat at the little store in the settlement. By now, of course, it's frozen; but maybe, to an animal wandering in the dark, it would still give off a smell.

My wife thinks I'm crazy. She doesn't even believe I really saw a tundra cat that other time. She says I'm just sitting here because of some morbid fantasy, shut up in my own world, and that it's my fault the rest of the family is stuck out here too. She doesn't understand about the tundra cat—not only its uniqueness, its being a species found only in Greenland, but also the role it played in the Inuit myths: a mythical being, its silence harboring—gracefully, nonchalantly—ultimate secrets. She doesn't understand that a person might be intrigued by this, might think it's worth sitting out here to …

Well, obviously her words have gotten under my skin, or I wouldn't keep going on like this. The air out here is bracing, the stars rigid, implacable. It's nice the way it's morning without being morning, a morning that allows the night to persist, to keep brooding about whatever it's brooding about. I think about the spreading miles of darkness, and beyond that, the ice plateau—a place so remote the mind balks at considering it. The solitude is so perfect that the slabs of meat on the wall almost seem like company.

# 3

November. No question of seal meat now—the last time I set some out, it got stuck so fast to the ice on the wall that I couldn't wrench it off, and during the "day"—the few hours of "day"—the little slabs were still there, and my wife said this looked so ridiculous (though just who would have been there to see them is unclear) we had to get rid of them. I didn't see what was so terrible about it—we recruited the kids to help us scrape and chip them off, a little family project; but Annette was really mad and forbade me, more or less, to put them there again. So now I have no enticements for a feline prowler; just my persistence and my hope that another one will come.

At least she can't accuse me of keeping "late hours"—I'm in the "predawn blackness" now, yet it's nine in the morning. Compared to last month it's even colder and—somehow—stiller. Spending so much time in this way, you learn that there's something the stars are keeping watch over, something in the stillness that's reticent to speak, yet could, if it were inclined; you don't know what it is, never will, but there's something.

Again, she's blaming me that we're all "stuck" here—as if it were really my fault. Having grown up in Newfoundland, it was natural for Annette and me—she was as much a part of the decision as I was— to be curious to cross the strait and spend some time here. I never guaranteed, I never signed anything that said I wouldn't get drawn in by the place and want to stay here awhile. I'd also like to know, if we were to go back to Canada now, exactly on what money she thinks we're going to live; but that's a different matter, it would lead us too far afield.

Sitting here facing this immense North, I know it will never give an answer to the inquiry I pose to it; even the cat was, at most, a gesture, tantalizing but not conclusive. Yet this is where I am; this is the direction I face.

# 4

Now, in December, it's dark twenty-four hours a day. It doesn't make any difference, either, what time of day I sit out here, since there's no dawn to wait for; so I do it at random times, while back in the cottage they mostly sleep.

The stars keep their vigil with a pure patience. A little while ago I went into the cottage to take a cup of tea; they were all deep in slumber. I lit my flashlight and scribbled on a piece of paper:

> Dark, you once disclosed to me
> A sight I scarcely hoped to see;
> Now in deadly fealty
> I sink into the sea
> Of utter night, negation,
> Obscured by that which brightened me.

I left it on the table, hoping against hope that Annette would read it.

# A Little Night Musing

MY EDITOR WAS supposed to arrive at dusk; but now it's already night and I assume he's gone off somewhere. Maybe to some other appointment. Something more important than old Temkin and his manuscript on Japan; or maybe he just forgot.

He was a nice young man, American, an immigrant. At first, polite, but a little standoffish with me; loosening up and indulging little smiles as he got used to me. And he was—I hope I can tell by now—a good editor. His comments seemed astute, his attitude genuinely serious, and his rewritten sentences seem to me, and also to Aliza, to read very well.

"Was." I speak of him as if I've already lost him. But he completely ignored his appointment, didn't even bother to call.

## 2

I haven't bothered turning on a light since I stopped working around dusk. The computer screen still glows. Here by the window, cold is seeping in; I haven't gone to get a sweater.

I cannot finish this project if he leaves. In Spanish, I can write without a personal editor; in English, I need someone to go over what I've done. I am eighty years old and cannot go looking for another editor if he leaves.

Yes, I could be overreacting. It's the first time he's done something like this, and part of my shock is because it's so unlike him. But on the other hand, he seemed peculiarly distant, detached, at the last meeting—as if he were losing interest; and I have a right to some anxiety after the way my first editor left.

My first editor, as it happens, did not lose interest gradually but announced to me one day out of the blue that she was finished. I did not expect it. It took me four months to find another editor. I had thought, in fact, that I was doing her a good turn by taking her on. She, too, was young, American; but a more recent immigrant, very much needing to find work. She was not even—I didn't want to admit it to myself then—a first-rate editor. She was also headstrong and couldn't allow that some of her revisions might be arbitrary. But I was happy with her and, I think, nice to her. I did not expect her to announce one afternoon without warning, after we had sat here for an hour going over a chapter, that she had found another job and couldn't continue with my book at all, not even in the evenings, not even a few hours here and there.

# 3

I hear Aliza in the kitchen. She probably thinks I'm still working, and so hasn't called in to me yet. I should get up and join her there.

Except that a certain immobility has crept in … I was an immigrant, too, like these editors, these young people. Fifty years ago, when a call came to me all the way in Santiago, I answered. The Hebrew University, here in Jerusalem, had just then decided to have a criminology department. They didn't feel, though, that among the local talent there was anyone sufficiently qualified to set it up; they needed someone from abroad. I wasn't the first on their list, but not so far down it, either; I didn't answer the call out of any objective need. No, I … answered the call. The Jewish state …

And I was well accommodated. Head of the department, large (though Spartan) office, diligent secretaries. What about Hebrew? I asked. They said it was all right, I could learn it. And I did—much faster than I expected. And now for fifteen years they've given me all the trappings of an emeritus, even a fund in my name to finance my trips to the Far East, pay my editors and typists; and I've finally written books—five altogether since retiring—that long ago in Santiago I would only dream of writing.

So then, what?

# 4

The country back then, the mid-1960s, was depressed and struggling. Still needing cash infusions from Jews abroad; still needing to find foreign professors for academic ballast.

Problems and all, though, I fused with it faithfully, accepted my calling. Stayed faithful when the Jordanian shells started thundering in Jerusalem, and on the stricken faces you saw the fear of another catastrophe, this time in Zion, meant to be a refuge from catastrophe. Stayed faithful in the even worse war six years later, when leaders who were already practically canonized as legends were revealed as little more than bumbling fools. I was already in the thick of it by then; the department was growing, and the stones, pines, and fragrant dusks of Jerusalem had already invaded and conquered the territory deep within me.

And so it has been. More wars, buses exploding in our streets, mind-boggling achievements, from desert to farms to helping usher humanity into a science-fiction world of computers and satellites, a world where your brother in Santiago smiles at you from a screen on your desk. Yes, the department thrived. I've seen generation after generation of young scholars eager to make their mark, hosted conferences of colleagues from abroad who sit gravely through the lectures and are then carted to the Holocaust museum and the Wall, then back to their luxury hotels. I became part of it ... yet at this moment feel myself to be part of very little.

## 5

Quiet—I've heard nothing from Aliza for a long time.

The fact is, not one of the books I've written here has been translated into Hebrew. I take that to be a fair indication of my real function here: to set up a department and give it a patina of prestige. It's not connected to the importance, if any, of the research I do. No, what's wanted is my name and the name of the university together on a dust jacket—in English. Do my studies of crime and punishment in Singapore, in Thailand, in Japan, have any pertinence to any of the issues here? No one will ever know, because my books remain foreign books, quarantined from the local discourse apart from a few prying scholars. And that is only a slight exaggeration.

And yet, does one have a right to ask for more—more than honor and convenience? All expenses paid for the work I keep doing doggedly till the end, however much it may be a sideshow by now, a relic?

Just, perhaps, some marker, something that would have said: "Israel Temkin was here."

## 6

Last spring my daughter Sylvia came from London for a visit. She brought with her Darien, her nice English lawyer, who wears wire-rim glasses, talks about our affairs with some familiarity, and is full of amiable interest in Jerusalem with its sites and sights. She also brought with her Reggie and Danny—nice English boys, who went in khaki shorts in the April warm spell, who even played with Yossi and Miri, children who live next door to us.

Sylvia enjoyed being able to use her Hebrew with us, and was a vivacious tour guide for her husband, still very proud of her old haunts. She slips back and forth between the two worlds, English and Hebrew—or should I say three, since she also knows some Spanish—very easily.

I did not ask any of this directly, but was able to gather that: They are not members of any Jewish institution like a synagogue (not surprising for a daughter of sworn secularists) or a school (for the boys). Darien, who used to talk about converting, apparently doesn't talk about it anymore. The smattering of Hebrew Reggie knows is because at first she made a point of using it with him; she has not continued the practice with Danny, for whom Hebrew is as foreign as Urdu.

This ship I've boarded ... I would say she's disembarked. The boys, in the future? I suppose something could happen ...

My editor was supposed to arrive at dusk; but now it's already so late at night that I can't even hope he'll still materialize. I should get up, turn off the machine, go out from this room. I shouldn't just stay here; but I do, staring out the window toward the street. Israel Temkin was here.

# Office Dreams

M Y OFFICE IS not a room, a bedroom, where someone sleeps. It doesn't know what I do before I arrive in the morning, or after I leave at night. It has never seen me sleep or have a dream. It doesn't even know I have a wife.

It only knows my waking, "working" self, and so it has to try to figure things out from what little it sees. It assumes, from the fact that I sit tinkering with other people's words, that I'm an editor, that this is my real work. It sees me stare out the window, drink coffee—or sit blankly a few moments, doing nothing at all; but it doesn't know what to infer from this. And what is my relationship with the women, the two or three women who drift in and out of the office a few times each day? It tries to decipher the subtle codes of glances, gestures, words, jokes; but it isn't sufficient, it's only an office and an office doesn't know what to make of such things.

AND WHAT DO I know about it?

When I arrive, after all, it's already bright morning, sunlight streaming through the window; and when I leave, it's still only late afternoon. I do not see my office in the hours before I arrive in the morning and after I leave for the day.

My office observes alone as the first grey dusk light wanders into the room; the daylight, ruffled, silently leaves. The desk, the shelves, the computer, the coat rack fall into deep, gloomy meditation. The darkness settles, outside, inside. All is dark.

It may seem that there is not very much for an office to do, to be aware of, through a long stock-still night. The only thing that moves is time. But perhaps, because the wait for dawn is so long, it dreams the event instead. In its dream-dawn, the sun first peeps up in the east as a rim of sparks in utter blackness. As it rises it does not dispel the dark, only fills it. It grows and grows like a crimson balloon, slowly swallowing the jet-black sky; till it bursts and pours into the office, flooding it in liquid light.

MY OFFICE DOES not know that I sleep in a bed at night with my wife. It cannot understand how we are very much together—twitching at each other's thoughts, frowning and muttering at each other's dreams; but also very much apart—sometimes sunk deep in dreams from which our hands can't reach even to each other.

It doesn't know that my real work is done out of the office, when I'm at home; and not only that, but when I'm asleep. Down in some dream a poem—which may be pure nonsense, inanity—starts in my head; I wake, it's dark, I make a mental note to remember it, record it carefully in consciousness … but by morning it's gone.

It doesn't know—or maybe it does—that I've dreamed about *it*. I've found myself inside it at night; have gone to the window where I, too, wait for dawn. But for me it remains only a dream—within the dream—of dawn; always, before anything happens, a voice summons me back, I wake and there are children's voices and morning, I look at my wife and for a moment could almost tell her that dawn is lost and we are banished and the world is not our home.

IN THE HOUR in the morning before I arrive, my office is alone with itself and the sunlight, and my poem is there, in the bright air. I walk in and it flees out the window like startled birds; and I settle into another day of effort and ignorance.

# A Thing of the Past

S HE STOOD WATCHING while they played basketball. Pete was aware of her—constantly; even when, his back to her, he shot the ball over an outstretched hand; or got jostled in a cursing, chuckling throng under the hoop.

She was from somewhere else; none of them knew her. She stood alone; small and, seemingly, determined about being there. That was, maybe, why he was so aware of her … he felt kind of sorry for her. You surmised that she wasn't such a great basketball fan, but wanted them to talk to her, wanted to meet them. And he knew that, with this particular group of guys, that wasn't too likely; none of them were the type that just goes up to strange girls and talks to them. Certainly not himself, however much it frustrated him. Yet in this case—maybe this was why he was so keyed to her—he feared that he would …

It was August; there was just enough shade on the court, from the trees around it, to make playing ball bearable in the late-afternoon heat. The game, last in a series of three-on-threes, ended—an 11-9 win for the other team, not Pete's. They all affably, chucklingly went on their ways, acting as if the girl wasn't there. They were all—Pete took note of it—really just going to leave her standing there, by herself. And it was with a cold feeling in the pit of his stomach that he sensed that he wouldn't do that, couldn't go along with it. (He was no less shy than they; but he felt sorry for her). And it was with a sense of inner alarm and amazement that he felt his legs walking toward where she stood, just beyond the sideline of the court; as if his legs were doing it, carrying him into something against his will …

She wore a white dress with a flower pattern, not too short; her arms and legs were pleasantly rounded; but not much chest. Her hair was long and thick, an auburn color; she watched him as if pleasantly surprised he'd decided to walk over to her.

"Hi," he said. He crossed the sideline and stood beside her, basketball tucked under his arm.

"Hi."

"You're from, uh … not around here?"

"I'm from Canada."

"*Canada*?"

"British Columbia."

She said it as if those words would clarify everything. She really didn't look bad—altogether. Big azure eyes, high cheekbones, small straight nose, small pursed lips; her voice was high, faintly British in inflection, and with intense r's and l's, as if she talked with a stiff tongue. (Yes, not much chest; but very curved from her waist out to her hips …)

"British Columbia. So … how'd you wind up in this place?"

"I'm visiting." Again, she pronounced this simply and clearly, as if it was enough to explain.

"Visiting … who you visiting?"

"My uncle. My uncle lives over there."

She gestured vaguely: toward the lawn sloping away from the court, the clubhouse and pool of the development that were there, the row of houses—not close but discernible—across the street from the clubhouse.

She said: "Can I ask you something?"

"Sure."

"What's your name?"

"Pete … What's yours?"

"Dawn."

He just looked at her; she'd again said it with that simple finality, and anyway, he didn't know what to say.

She said: "Pete, Dawn. They're both nature-names."

"*What?*"

"You know, Pete, peat?"

"What, you mean like peat moss? ... I once had a friend who called me Pete Moss."

"A friend called you that?"

"Yeah."

"Well, he was imaginative."

"Yeah, I guess so."

"Can I have that please?"

He stared dumbly at her pointing finger, and it took him a while to realize she meant his basketball. When he gave it to her she dribbled it—flat-palmed like a girl—over to the basket, clutched it with both hands, and heaved up a shot that barely grazed the rim.

Pete—tall, with thick, longish brown hair, a craggy face but with gentle, well-formed eyes and mouth—ambled over; relieved, actually, to be able to move, to be doing something.

She was picking up the ball from where it had rolled toward the left corner; she heaved up another shot. This one only grazed the net beneath the rim.

Pete trotted over rightward of the basket and retrieved the ball; bent his knees lazily and tossed up a shot that swished through cleanly.

"Smarty pants," she said. The ball rolled over toward her; she picked it up and held it, looking at him.

She was flushed from the exertion, eyes bright; it looked good, actually.

"So you're on your school team?" she said, eyes bright, as he walked up and again stopped—not too close to her.

"I was. I was on JV."

"JV. So you were in *tenth*."

"Yeah. In a couple of weeks ... the wonderful world of eleventh grade."

"Well I'm going into twelfth."

"Yeah?" he said. "Where do you live over there in British Columbia?"

"I live in Fort St. John," she said. But this time not with the pert finality; instead, looking at him, as if aware this would perplex him.

"Fort St. John. What's that?"

"It's a real small town up in the north. The boondocks."

"So you're from the boondocks?"

"You could say that."

"Been in the States before?"

"Just once. When I was younger."

"What do you think of it?"

"I think it has a lot of great basketball players."

"Yeah?"

She looked funny holding the ball, her small hands making it look bigger than it was. He had the idea to go up and playfully bat it away from her; but he didn't. It seemed it would be too forward, and it wasn't the sort of thing he did.

Instead he looked at his watch. "So ... they're probably waiting for me for supper."

"OK."

"You doing anything tonight?"

"Not sure. Let me check my appointment book." She laughed. "Of course not."

"Uh ... want to go for a walk around here?"

"OK."

"Like ... eight-thirty, something like that."

"OK."

"So, where do I pick you up?"

Lying on his bed, he still heard them out in the kitchen. He'd come home; showered; then joined them for the meal. His older sister said something about going out tonight. So that they wouldn't get ideas—they sometimes asked him to baby-sit for his little sister—he said: "I'm going out too."

"Oh," said his mother. "Someplace with Mike?"

"No ... it's with a girl."

"Oh," his mother said. "Someone we know?"

"No ... someone I met. She's from Canada."

"Canada!" his mother said. "Petie's quite the man about town lately."

Although, as usual, he wished she wouldn't talk the way she did, he didn't really mind her mentioning it. It *was* pretty cool; the second girl he'd had something with this summer. His older sister seemed tuned out, indifferent; his little sister gazed with bright, enthused curiosity; his father munched his food slowly, thoughtfully.

But he'd excused himself, before dessert; because he didn't want to sit there anymore, wanted to be alone already. And now he lay on his bed in the dark, still hearing them out there; windows open on the night. It was almost night, one bird still singing.

It was totally and perfectly still. The house wasn't in the development; it was about a ten-minute trek from it down Clifton Park Center Road where it intersected with Moe Road. It was a one-story brick house under trees, not large, so that you were never far from the others and could mostly hear them. Living out here always made him feel a bit different; all of his friends lived in the development. Actually, they—his family—*were* different; more cultured. His older sister played classical piano; his father was a psychologist and read all kinds of books. He, too, used to read all kinds of books. But when he turned twelve, he asked his parents to take his bookcases out of his room; and they did, moving them down to the cellar. He didn't want his friends to come in and think he was some sort of bookworm; he wanted them to think he was a cool person, a basketball player.

The bird was still singing beautifully, very solitary now in the dark. He was going out to meet a girl again. So soon after Laurie. It was amazing ... He still didn't know why ten days ago, when he called Laurie and her sister answered, Laurie had barely agreed to come to the phone and then had snubbed him so coldly. "What, you've got no days this week?" "No." "What, so we're not doing stuff together at all anymore?" "No." There was a deterioration before that, but he didn't think the stone would hit the bottom so bluntly ... But here he was again. Back on his feet. No, this girl—Dawn—wasn't as pretty as Laurie. But she was a girl, and she'd said "OK" to all of his questions.

He realized he was wishing for something … what was it? He was wishing one of his friends, Mike or Wally, would call so that he could tell him, no, he couldn't hang out tonight—and why. But they didn't.

To HIS SURPRISE and dread, she asked him in. She'd changed into a short-sleeved green blouse with a frilly front, white pants; a touch more formal than an American girl—or at least the ones he knew—would have worn.

He had to ascend steps, stand in a bright living room and be introduced to her uncle, her aunt, and some other people, he couldn't follow who they were. They all seemed like stern, stuffy people, and standing there in his T-shirt, jeans, and sneakers—someone who was about to take the niece out into the night—he didn't feel at all comfortable. But he seemed to pass the inspection. The aunt said: "Come home at a reasonable hour, Dawnie."

It WAS AN August night in Clifton Knolls, a development in Clifton Park, New York. Warm and—though it was a weeknight—surprisingly still and quiet considering it was summer and kids were home from school. Sprinklers gurgled in yards and the sound of crickets rang. The stars, newly dawned, were already clear and bright.

They'd turned left from Locust Lane, where her uncle's house stood facing the clubhouse-pool-courts complex, and were going slowly down Beechwood Drive, past the houses with their open garages and light spilling from their front windows. He knew where he was taking her, though he didn't say.

For a while neither of them had said anything, and he was relieved when at last she talked.

She said: "So. How is it that a handsome basketball player like you doesn't have a girlfriend somewhere?"

"Oh … I had one."

"Had one?"

"Yeah … Laurie … it ended about ten days ago. Don't really know why."

She didn't answer. More or less to fill the silence, he said: "Some friends set me up with her. I didn't really know her. I don't know. Maybe I still don't." He said: "I've got this bottle of vodka. Was thinking of bringing it tonight, but I decided not to."

"*Vodka?*"

"Yeah. It's hidden behind my house."

"Well. You could have drunk it. I'm not much of a drinker."

"We'd have had to dodge cop cars."

"Oh. That doesn't sound like fun."

"No. I figured you wouldn't be crazy about it." He said: "So what's it like, up in your town? Must get freezing in winter."

"Oh yes. Freeezing."

"Is it really small?"

"Yes, it's very small. And people get bored. At least, they complain about boredom all the time. I guess I'm lucky, because I don't get bored."

"You don't get bored?"

"No."

"Why not?"

"Well ... I love to read so much, I guess it keeps me busy."

Some kids were approaching them—Russ Nedell and a couple of his friends. Pete didn't like Russ. To try and keep him friendly, so he wouldn't say something malicious, he said: "Hey, Russ."

"Hey!" Russ said. "Korman!"

That was all; Russ and his friends passed them, though they were looking at them, especially at Dawn.

He said: "You read a lot?"

"Yes. A lot."

"What kind of things?"

"Well ... I love Jane Austen. And Tolstoy. These long novels ... I just get totally absorbed in them."

"Yeah? I used to read too."

"*Used* to?" He felt her looking at him quizzically in the dark.

Up ahead he could already make out the part of Beechwood where the houses gave out and there was just a steel fence on either side; beyond the fence, on both sides, the murky darkness where the waters of the pond were. Out there, on the right side of the road, a half-moon had risen.

He said: "Yeah, I read a lot when I was little. Westerns, American history, I don't know ..."

He had to stop; feelings had welled up inside him, surprisingly forceful.

He said: "These days, I don't know ... I don't seem to find time for it."

"Well. I guess we have something in common. Or we *did*."

He laughed. "Yeah." He said: "I write stuff, too."

"You write?"

"Yeah."

"What sort of writing?"

"I don't know. I just write junk in my notebook when something happens to me that's intense."

"That sounds nice. But why do you say junk?"

"Oh, I don't know, it's just ..."

"You're always putting yourself down, Pete Moss."

He kept walking a bit stiffly; one side of his mouth curled up in a smile.

He said, finally: "First of all, my name's not Pete Moss. Second, what do you mean, always putting myself down."

"You're always saying ... I just write junk. I don't know ... I guess I'm just ... I don't know ..."

He was silent; but he was grinning broadly.

He said: "Well, call it modesty."

"*Yes*! Modesty, of course. A great virtue."

They walked on in silence, as if what she'd said was too profound for further comment.

They'd gone past the houses now and, walking on the left side of the road, were beside the dark expanse of the golf course, guarded by the fence. It seemed to him that her hand grazed his.

He said: "This is the golf course on the left. Sort of a hangout."

"A *hang*out."

"Yeah. Kids go there at night to drink beer and stuff. The cops never go there. They drive around in the streets, but they never bother with the golf course." He said: "We could go there."

"*We* could?"

"Yeah ... if you feel like it."

"Do we have to play golf?"

"Nah ... I'm lousy at it anyway."

Now she laughed, sudden and high.

They were approaching the part of Beechwood where it veered sharply left, following the fence. The land around them now looked flat and murky, faintly lit, as if they'd left the development and were in some sort of marshland.

He said, as they were veering left: "So how long are you here for?"

"In America?"

"Yeah."

"Four more days."

"Four more *days*? Not very much."

"Let's see, tonight's ... Thursday? So I have to fly back on Monday ... I'm only here for a week. I wish I'd gone out to the courts and met you sooner. Just sitting at my uncle and aunt's, I got bored."

"*Bored*?"

She laughed. "Yes. Even I. With my friends so far away." She said: "But we can get together again. If you want."

He said: "Sure."

They walked on mutely, and came, at the end of this stretch of the fence, to the gate of the golf course. He stopped before it. She stopped too, not realizing, of course, that it was here.

He said: "This is the gate. It's usually unlocked."

He pushed it; it opened, with a creak.

"So," he said. "Want to play some golf?"

DARK AND HUSHED as always, a place brooding by itself, separate from the world of the road. To their right—he was leading her to a specific spot—were the tall trees along a little inlet of the pond; ahead were the tall trees along the pond itself.

They came to the edge of the pond; obscured behind the thick, dark leaves.

He turned toward her.

Her face, in the faint moonlight, looked distant and pale.

He wanted to say: "I used to take Laurie here"; but didn't.

She said: "Can I ask you something?"

He stared at her.

"Sure."

She said: "That guy we passed before?"

"Oh, Russ?"

"Yeah, him … What did he call you?"

"Call *me*?"

"Yes. What did he call you?"

He said: "Korman."

"*Korman*?"

"Yeah."

He said, "It's a Jewish name."

She was looking at him with some kind of expression.

She said—still looking at him that way: "*Jewish*. I can't believe it. I have *never* known a Jewish person before."

He said: "Well. Now you do."

She was still looking at him.

She said: "Pete Moss Korman."

He reached out and held her smooth, cool arms.

# 2

Coming back to the house at eleven-thirty, he was relieved that it was totally dark; they'd all gone to bed. His parents always watched the eleven-o'clock news in the breezeway; sometimes they kept watching after that, too. But not tonight, he saw, as he approached the breezeway from the driveway. He wouldn't have wanted to talk to anyone or explain anything.

To the left of the breezeway, as you faced the house, there used to be a garage; but years ago they'd had it converted into two rooms, his older sister's in front, his own in back. His sister's room was dark now too; as was the rest of the house, where his parents' and little sister's bedrooms were.

He got undressed and lay down on his bed, but never entertained any thought of sleeping. For one thing, he never slept at night in the summer, only here and there during the day. For another, even if he ever *did* sleep at night in the summer, he wouldn't have been able to now.

INSTEAD—AS ALWAYS at this hour—he turned on his radio, very softly so it wouldn't disturb his sister, to WRPI. It was the station of a nearby university; it played progressive rock as well as other kinds of music he was starting to get intrigued by.

This was the hour for a DJ who usually played some of the best soft, lyrical songs of the era, and tonight he didn't disappoint. "Sisotowbell Lane," "How Do You Feel" (so perfect ...), Steve Noonan's version of "Buy for Me the Rain," and above all, "Guinevere." He lay with his eyes closed. All the songs—every note, every chord—was connected to what had just happened. He took it all in ...

At two o'clock the late-night DJ came on. He played a live version of "Dark Star," a live version of "A Love Supreme"; then a long, live raga by Ravi Shankar. Now they were floating—still in the grass by the pond, but floating—through space. He and Dawn ...

AT DAWN HE went out through the breezeway into the backyard. Though the light was still faint, the birdsong was astonishingly loud. To the left was the lilac hedge (the lilacs of May long gone now in dry August), in front of him a short stretch of grass. It ended in, on the left, a woodshed that was behind the lilac hedge, and to the right of the woodshed, a line of trees. Behind that there was another stretch of grass, and then the woods.

The woodshed, and the trees, looked dark and somber now in the spectral light. Walking out in the yard, the dew soaked through his slippers. He saw their cat, Charlie, step out from the woodshed where he'd been sleeping on a burlap sack, sit at its entrance and contemplate the scene.

He walked till he could see, to the right, where the yard ended at Moe Road; across the road, the cornfield of the farm that was there. Over the cornfield, where it culminated in the just-visible farmhouses, there was a band of lavender light.

He stood gazing at it, birdsong resonating around him.

ABOUT NINE O'CLOCK he was jostled out of a doze by noise from the kitchen, and—not because he had any interest in eating—he went out there. Trudging up the steps from the breezeway, he saw his little sister, Abby, sitting at the table, his mother moving around preparing things.

"Well!" his mother said, gazing at him. "Look who's here!"

He stood there, rubbing his eyes.

"So!" she said. "How did your evening go?"

"Fine," he said. "Uh … is there some coffee?"

"Well," she said, "I *think* I could produce some to go with your pancakes."

He said: "No, that's OK. Just, uh … just the coffee."

"*What*?!" said Abby. "Petie doesn't want *pancakes*?"

"Uh, just call me when it's ready, OK?" he said, trudging backward down the steps.

HE TOLD THEM there was something special on the radio and took the steaming cup back to his room, shutting the door.

A ray of sun was streaming in through the window over his desk, the one that looked out on the side yard and Clifton Park Center Road. Charlie, curled at a lower corner of the bed, was bathed in sun; he appeared both ecstatic and deeply asleep.

He sat down on the bed; set the cup on the little stand, next to the radio.

He put his face deep in his hands.

No, he couldn't believe it, couldn't believe what was happening …

They'd planned to meet again tonight. Tomorrow, Saturday, her uncle and aunt were taking her to see other relatives in Massachusetts— in a certain place there, she couldn't remember its name. But they'd planned to meet again on Sunday, too—before she flew back on Monday.

Two more nights when—this, too, they'd agreed on—they'd go to the golf course, to the place by the pond.

He felt that something was streaming onto him, engulfing him—like Charlie; but it wasn't the sun. As for her flying home on Monday—he couldn't think about it. It wasn't real to him.

ABOUT ELEVEN O'CLOCK the phone rang in the little foyer outside his and his sister's rooms.

He went out, picked up the receiver, said: "Hello?"

"Hello?"

"*Dawn?* ... Hi."

"Hi. How are you?"

"I'm great."

"How'd you sleep?"

"Well ... I didn't."

"You didn't sleep?"

"No. I don't sleep at night in the summer."

"Not at all?"

"No, I don't know, I, I can't ... How about you?"

"Well ... not that much either."

"Yeah ... there was a lot to think about, I guess."

As he was talking, he was taking the phone into his room, shutting the door on the cord, and sitting down at the edge of his bed—as far as the cord would allow when he did this.

She said: "I'm *so* upset."

He frowned.

"What? Why?"

"Well, you're not going to believe this ... While we were out, my parents called. They wanted to talk to me. So Uncle Trevor and Aunt Mabel explained where I was. And my father ... got very mad."

"Got mad." He sat, perched stiffly, uncomfortably on the bed. "Why?"

"Oh, because I was out with a *strange boy*. Because they let me out with a *strange boy*."

"Oh."

"My father is sometimes infuriating. They told him that they met you, and that you're very nice. But he wouldn't listen to them. The only thing he could think of was the word *strange*."

"Oh, boy."

"So he told them—this is the ruling from on high—that I'm not to go out with you at night again while I'm here. I'm *so* upset."

He sat very still. "Oh. Really?"

"But—it's all right with him if you come here to the house and visit me. I'm sorry. I know it isn't much. I guess we could sit in my room and talk. If you don't want to, I understand."

He said: "No … that sounds OK."

"It's OK?"

"Yeah … at least we could be together."

He heard her sigh with relief. "Yes … I *so* want to see you again."

"Well … I do too."

There was a lull.

"Would seven-thirty this evening or so be all right? That's about when we've finished up with dinner here, and … we'd have some time."

"That sounds fine."

"All right … Well … at least something. I guess."

"Yeah. I guess so."

"So how are you?"

"I'm great … Like I said, I couldn't sleep. So I went out for a walk in the morning. I mean, really early, when it was just getting light."

"You went for a *walk*?"

"Yeah. It's pretty around here. Especially at that hour."

"It's a country place, you said?"

"Yeah, kind of. It's not far from the development, but it's already farm country."

She said: "You know what? I hear Aunt Mabel down there getting lunch ready. We have guests, so I should help her."

"OK."

"I'm sorry I can't talk more now. Is it OK? I'm so happy at least we'll see each other tonight."

"Sure … I am too."

"So seven-thirty's OK, then?"

"Yeah. fine."

"All right. I'm sorry about my father. What … what can I do."

"It's all right."

"Bye."

"Bye."

"See you later."

"OK."

BUT THINGS SEEMED to keep going wrong. It turned out his parents were going out tonight—to a dinner honoring the retiring principal of the nearby school where his father worked. As for his older sister, Wendy, she was going to a party she said she'd been planning on for a week. Pete, mentioning that he was supposed to see the Canadian girl again, asked if a girl who sometimes baby-sat Abby could come tonight. But when his mother called her, she had other plans.

Standing again in the entrance to the kitchen, in the late afternoon while his parents were having their coffee at the table, a ray of late-afternoon sun cascading through the backyard trees and flooding the red-and-white-checked tablecloth, he told them that the girl was flying back to Canada on Monday and going to Massachusetts tomorrow, and it was important that he meet with her. He could see that they took it seriously. Finally his mother suggested that, instead of him visiting her at her uncle and aunt's house, she could visit him here, at their house, while he was baby-sitting.

He called Dawn—happy to have any reason to call her, to hear her voice—and explained this suggestion to her. In a procedure that wasn't at all simple, which involved her uncle and aunt calling her parents in Fort St. John, she got an answer of yes. Her father asked her, through her uncle, if Pete's parents would be there while she was visiting. She said yes.

He lay down on his bed again. There were just a few birds chirping now, sounding tired and pensive in the heat. He thought of writing about what was happening; but he was too worn-out, and anyway it was all too new and stupefying. He realized that what had seemed like a string of bad, perverse luck had ended in some good luck. Now, when they got together, it would be in a house where there were no grownups. Though it still wasn't as good as the pond.

## 3

Again the hour of nightfall, with one bird—possibly the same one—continuing to sing by itself after all others had stopped. Wendy—in her usual last whirl of activity and words—had left for her party. His parents, much more quietly, had left for their dinner. He, just now in Abby's room, had explained to her the terms: she could play for another half-hour, then had to brush her teeth and go to bed.

It was ten to eight; Dawn was supposed to arrive at eight. Now, on his bed, he thought how at this time yesterday, too, he'd been here, thinking about Dawn ... but in such a different way. He remembered that he'd been thinking about the word *two*—two girls in one summer, in quick succession. About how Laurie—he'd thought then—was prettier than Dawn; even wishing—apart from the "two"—that it was Laurie he was going out to meet, to take to the pond, instead of Dawn.

And now ... What was happening to him? How he could feel this way, after being with her once? Did he really know her? No, he didn't really even know her; how was it possible, after being with her for a few hours all told, mostly in the dark? Yet soon she was coming here, to his house.

He heard the car pull up in the driveway, and thought: what an idiot. Why hadn't he left more lights on, instead of just the breezeway light and Abby's—to make it look as if people, such as his parents, were home? True, one of their cars was still in the driveway. But what if it wasn't enough, and they suspected? Or what if, anyway, they wanted to accompany Dawn to the door and meet his parents?

He lay tense and still.

But when the knock came on the front breezeway door, it sounded soft, diffident, and solitary.

He swiveled up from the bed, flicked on his light as he passed it, went out to the breezeway door.

She stood there in a sleeveless pink top and jeans. Her hair looked different—bigger, more fluffed-out. (How could he not have thought she was beautiful?)

He said: "Hi, come in."

She stepped in, smiling shyly.

He said: "Find the place OK?"

"Oh—yes," she said. "My uncle seems to know his way around here. Makes sense, I guess."

"I was a jerk. I should have left more lights on."

She frowned. "What?"

"More lights on, so … My parents aren't home, you know. They already left."

"Oh. Oh. Actually my uncle said it was kind of dark. But I don't think he meant anything by it. I don't think they suspected anything."

"No?"

"No, I don't think so."

She smiled at him.

He felt he should touch her. Instead he said: "I can show you my abode."

"OK," she said. "Fine."

STEPPING INTO THE room, he went and sat on the bed.

She went in a few steps, stood looking around her.

There wasn't much for her to see. To her right, the bed; behind it the closet; before her his desk, beneath the side window; to the left the wall where his bookcase once stood, now with only a map of the world, a print of Van Gogh's *Barques au Saint-Marie*, a watercolor of a vase by his mother, and beneath these, his record cabinet with his turntable and speakers on it.

She stepped up to the desk, took down a bowling trophy that was on the windowsill above it.

She held it—a gold, graceful bowler atop a gold column; he saw her arms, her shape …

She said: "Did you win this?"

"That?" He sat back on his hands. "Yeah, it was in some contest, when I was eleven or something."

"Well," she said, setting it on the sill and turning to look at him with a smile. "You're quite the athlete."

"Oh, I don't know. I might not even make varsity basketball this year. Or I might make it, but sit on the bench all the time. I don't know if it would be worth it."

"Well," she said. "I thought you looked really good yesterday."

"Yeah," he said—sitting forward again, resting his forearms on his legs, "but those weren't such good players I was playing with. Not the best ones, anyway."

She looked at him in a certain way.

He said: "I know, putting myself down again."

She smiled; then looked at a place on the bed, came over and sat on it—but not too close, a few feet to his right. Still he didn't touch her. After last night, he didn't think it would be this way. Why did he feel as if he had to start from the beginning again?

She sunk her face in her hands.

When her face emerged again, her expression was complex, a little harried.

She said: "I just wanted to say. Those things I was saying about my father before … I didn't mean to imply that he's a bad person or something. He's not. He makes me angry, but I guess you could say that he means well." She said: "He's a very religious Catholic. It makes him very … uptight."

"Yeah, I can see that."

She said—as if she hadn't heard him: "You know what I think? I think he uses it as a cover. He has all kinds of fears. That people might go out and … experience things, God forbid. He uses religion as a cover for that, I think, to justify it."

He sat back on his hands again, contemplated this; he had no idea what to say.

She said—intensely within her thoughts: "The effect—on me—is to push me away from the religion. I mean, I might be attracted to some aspects of it. But the way he is … I don't know, it pushes me away."

He said: "Yeah, I can understand that."

She sat, deep in thought.

When she looked at him again, she had a complex but different light in her blue eyes.

"And you … are Jewish."

He smiled, nodded. "That's right."

She kept looking at him.

"And you *don't* have Jesus."

He shrugged and shook his head. "Guess not."

She let her gaze wander forward again.

"I've always found it fascinating. I've *always* wanted to know more about the Jewish people. And yet I've never known any. It always seemed so—abstract to me."

"Well," he said. "I can understand that. Except for my family, I don't really know any Jewish people either."

She looked at him.

"How can that be?"

"Well. There aren't any in Clifton Park either, except for us."

She said: "That must be lonely."

He considered this. "Yeah, it is in a way."

She said: "There's a lot about you that's lonely, Pete boy. Pete Moss."

He looked away from her; he tried to smile, as if what she was saying wasn't too serious.

She said: "So how did this happen?"

He brightened, faintly. "What?"

"That you're the only Jewish family here."

"Oh. My parents were in New York City. My father found a job as psychologist in one of the schools around here, so they had to move here. That was really the only reason."

She said: "Did they have you yet?"

"No. They had my older sister. They were just starting out, I guess."

"So you've always been—here?"

"Yeah."

There was a silence. In it, he heard all that he hadn't said—about how they weren't, originally, from New York City, but had come there from Vienna on boats, with their parents, in the late 1930s; it stood in the silence.

They heard something from the other end of the house.

She said: "Who's that?"

He said: "That's my little sister, getting ready for bed."

She seemed to mull this.

"Are you going to tuck her in?"

"Nah ... She likes to do it herself now. She's into this independence thing. She's very proud of it."

They heard Abby close the bathroom door behind her; then her own door; then silence.

He reached out and took her forearm; he tugged lightly.

She came over beside him; they kissed, awkwardly.

He tried to move her down, with him, onto the bed; but she kept sitting there.

She said: "I feel funny."

He said—sitting back up again: "Why?"

"About your sister."

"Oh."

He said: "I'll close the door."

"No." She said: "Does she fall asleep?"

"Yeah. She falls asleep fast. She knows she can come here if she needs me for something. But she never does." He said: "I'll close the door."

"No—wait." She said: "I need a little more time."

"Oh … OK."

He said: "How much time do we have, by the way?"

"How much time?"

"Yeah—till they come and pick you up."

"Oh … They're supposed to come at about ten."

"*Ten?*"

They both looked at the clock of the radio, on the stand beside the bed; it said eight-twenty.

She said—with effort: "I want to say something."

He sat very still.

She turned toward him.

She said: "Yesterday. At the court. I was *so* happy when you came over and talked to me."

He touched her.

She said: "When I was watching you guys play … I was really watching you."

"Yeah?" he said.

She looked down in front of her again, as if troubled.

She seemed to need to muster herself to turn toward him again.

She said: "Last night meant something to me. It wasn't just a, 'I'm far from home, might as well have fun' thing. I felt much more than that."

He said: "Well, I did too, even though I'm not far from home."

She said—not seeming to hear him: "It wasn't the first time I've ever been in a situation like that. But I felt much more about it. It … *really* meant something to me."

He said: "Dawn, it meant a lot to me too." He said: "What are we going to do?"

She said—genuinely puzzled: "What?"

"You're leaving on Monday."

"Oh." She said: "I thought … we can talk about that on Sunday." She said: "Is that OK? We'll talk about it on Sunday?"

"Yeah. OK."

# 4

BUT WAKING UP at about eleven, after dozing off in the early morning, he felt as if a weight was oppressing him. It wasn't just the way his head felt from so little sleep. The mood from before—lying beside his radio all night—was gone, replaced by something else.

As he moved around, went out and took a cup of coffee, he realized what it was: that, after tomorrow, she'd be gone.

Yes, they had tomorrow evening together—in her room, with her uncle and aunt in the house. But that—the fact they wouldn't be able to do much—wasn't what weighed on him; what had already happened was amazing enough. It was that after tomorrow evening— what was left?

THERE WAS ONE lucky thing—he had the record.

Back in his room, he took it out of the cabinet, put it on the turntable, held the needle over the track; lowered it studiously to a spot toward the end of the song where the guitar ended and the banjo came in—just right.

He strode back to his bed so he could listen to it with his eyes closed:

> Soon she's going to fly away,
> Sadness is her own;
> Give herself a bath of tears
> And go home, and go home …

He played it several more times, not sure if it was making him feel better or worse.

IN THE EVENING he went for a walk in the streets of Clifton Knolls with his friend Mike. He'd already, of course, told Mike about Dawn on the phone. Mike had reacted grumpily. He'd been like that lately;

things were getting ragged with his girlfriend of two years, Pattie, on top of the trouble he always had with his father—all the worse since his mother had died some years ago.

Pete took his bottle of vodka with him. He'd bought it from an older guy a few weeks ago; he had to retrieve it from where he'd hidden it in the woods behind his house, the trees around him sedate and grave as sentinels in the dusk.

He and Mike passed it back and forth, sipping; when they saw the bubble-light of a cop car approach, they had to dash onto whatever lawn they were beside so the cops wouldn't see them. It was a typical Saturday night in the Knolls. Here and there music came from a party in a house; sometimes other groups of kids passed them.

As they got drunk, Mike began to talk.

"Yeah, Pete. Pattie and Dawn ... they're gonna leave us, pal. And you know what? They're gonna regret it. Pattie, she'll be with her Italian cook from the restaurant. Dawn ... she'll be with some lumberjack up there. And after a couple of years, you know what they're gonna say? How the hell did I get myself tied up with these empty-headed bastards when I could have been with guys like Pete Korman and Mike Niles? And you know what? It's gonna be good for them. They're gonna learn from it. They're gonna understand how good it was for them to be with us. They'll understand it too late, because it's gonna be too late for them, but they'll understand that it was better for them to be with guys like us, guys like Pete Korman and Mike Niles, guys who've got a lot inside, instead of these empty-headed bastards. That chef-bastard, you know what he does? He goes right up and pinches her ass through her cute little waitress uniform. And she's like ... oh, he's paying attention to me."

He took something more than a sip, almost a swig.

"Yeah, but Mike," Pete said. "Dawn, you know, she's gotta go back, she's got no choice."

"Ah, Pete." He lowered the bottle, sighing heavily. "You really believe that, do you, my man? I'm sorry if you're that naïve, pal. Don't you think, if she really wanted to, she could stay here somehow? Pete, you gotta understand—they leave us. They don't know what they have when they have us, and so they go to be with some guy who cooks good spaghetti. But in the end they're going to understand that it was a mistake. They'll understand that they should never have left guys like us …"

TOWARD ELEVEN THEY parted where Hemlock Drive gave out on Clifton Park Center Road. Mike, after a volley of loud statements and claps to Pete's shoulder, started back to his house in the Knolls. Pete, turning right, started the trek to his house at the Moe Road intersection.

It was darker and quieter out here than in the Knolls. The houses were fewer, between them patches of woods. Sometimes dogs howled from yards. Tonight a yellow moon shone through the trees. He let his right foot swing out over the roadside grass, trying to make a circular, rhythmic motion; realized he was doing it and stopped.

He took out the bottle from where he'd stashed it inside his shirt. He could just see that there was only a little vodka left, sloshing around at the bottom. On the one hand, he wanted to drink it; on the other, the thought of drinking any more of it made him feel sick.

He flung the bottle into the roadside ditch; he heard it clunk there without shattering.

He sang—in a low, dull voice, letting his feet make a sort of thumping rhythm:

> Soon she's gonna fly away,
> Sadly seeks her home;
> Give herself a…daffodil,
> And go ho-, ho-ho-home, ho-ho-home …

He said: "Dawnie baby, goddamit. You gotta be here with *me*."

His feet kept trudging heavily; he stopped, blinked off a wave of dizziness.

Starting again, he sang:

> I wanna be with a cinnamon girl,
> I can be happy … rest o' my life
> With a cinnamon girl.
> A dreamer o' pictures,
> I run in the night;
> You see us together
> Chasing the moonlight,
> My cinnamon girl …

He said: "Dawnie baby … Dawnie baby …"

THE LIGHT WAS on in the breezeway. Stepping in—rubbing his forehead and blinking—he saw his parents, watching TV with their glasses on, sitting beside each other on the couch.

"Hi," he said.

"Petie," said his mother. "Dawn called. She said it's urgent."

"*What?*"

His mother reached over to the TV and turned down the volume.

"*Dawn* called. She said it's urgent and you should call her no matter how late. That you should call her whenever you come in."

THE DOOR TO Wendy's room was open and it was dark in there, meaning she wasn't there. He took the phone, hauled it roughly into his room; turned on the light, closed the door on the cord, went and plopped heavily at the edge of the bed.

He started to dial; stopped, realizing he wasn't sure he really remembered the number.

Where was the number? On his desk somewhere …?

He decided to keep dialing; if he got it wrong, so someone would get a call at eleven-thirty at night.

"Hello?"

It was Dawn's voice.

"Dawn?"

"*Pete* … Oh, I'm so glad you called."

"What's up?"

"Oh … a lot."

"How was Massachusetts?"

"Oh, it was nice. How was your evening?"

"Uh, great. I was out with Mike."

"I know. Your mother told me."

"My mother … oh, you mean when you talked to her."

"Pete, you're not going to believe this."

She sounded close to tears.

She said: "I have to go back tomorrow."

"What? Tomorrow?"

"My father … changed the flight."

"What?"

"My father changed the flight from Monday to tomorrow."

"Oh, God. Why did he do that?"

"Oh, supposedly because of some school registration on Monday I'm supposed to go to …"

She stopped; he thought he heard a soft sob.

"Dawn?"

"It's not … of course it's not that. That's just a stupid thing. I could always have taken care of it."

"What is it then?"

"Oh … I'm sure my uncle called him."

"Called him about what?"

"Oh, you know … about … last night."

"Last night … about the lights not being on, right?"

She said nothing.

"You see, I told you, I'm an idiot. I'm an idiot."

"Pete—sweetheart—it's all right."

Her use of the word made him fall silent.

She said: "We've been together, right? Two times or three times, what difference does it make? We've been together, right?"

"Right. Of course."

"I'll miss you ..."

He heard her sob.

He had to sit and wait while she sobbed. He slapped his hand to his forehead.

"Pete ... I'll write as soon as I get there. OK? I'll write to you?"

"Of course."

"And ... will you write to me? *Please*? You'll answer me?"

"Dawn, how could you ask me like that? Of course I will."

"You *will* answer?"

"Dawn ..."

She said something muffled he couldn't hear.

"What?"

"*What* is your address?"

"Oh ... You got something to write with?"

"Yes."

"Pete Korman ... Clifton Park Center Road ... RD2 ... Elnora, New York ... 12065 ... USA." He said: "Got it?"

"Yes." She said: "I can't talk more. I'm too upset."

"OK."

"I just want to say ... I had a *wonderful, wonderful* time here. Thank you sweetie."

"Of course."

"Thank you ... I'll write ... Bye."

"Bye."

He put the receiver back in its place; sat there numb.

How could he not have said more to her?

# 5

And after a little more than a week a letter came from her, addressed to "Peter Coreman," written in a blue, beautiful, flowing hand on magenta stationery. Opening with "Dearest Pete," she told him about the flight back, how miserable she felt, how she couldn't look at Lake Ontario and the wheat fields because it meant Canada—away from him. She told him what it was like to get back, how she could only be "coldly polite" with her father, how good it was to see her friends again, how she told them what a great—though all too short—time she'd had in America.

Toward the end she wrote:

> And now I want to tell you about something not too pleasant that happened. I mentioned to my best friend, Elinor, that you're Jewish, and she reacted by saying something nasty that I don't even want to repeat to you. I was very upset, but we were on the phone and I didn't say anything. I haven't told you, of course, because we haven't had time, that I get very upset when I hear things like that. This may sound strange, but at those moments, at least, it makes me feel that I want to get closer to the Jewish people and maybe even be one of them.
>
> I'm thinking of how I can talk about this with Elinor, but I think it would be best to wait till I've calmed down and am less upset. I don't think it would accomplish anything to try and talk with her about it while I'm still so disturbed about how she chose to express herself.
>
> And now, Pete dear, I want to end, of course, on a more positive note. I want to tell you again what a wonderful time I had, how <u>simply wonderful</u> it is to be with you. I so wish we could have had more time together, but I'm grateful for the time we did have. And…I want to know what's new! Has school started yet? I want so much to hear from you, so <u>write soon!</u>
>
> Much, much love,
>
> Dawn

He looked for a long time at that closing; and when he was in his room, where the letter was, he kept returning to it and gazing at it.

HE ANSWERED HER letter after a day. He told her that, yes, school had started and it looked like another boring year, particularly in social studies where it turned out his teacher was the notoriously mind-numbing Miss Valvo. He told her a little about Mike, how distressed he was now that Pattie had finally, definitively left him; he didn't tell her how much he and Mike had been drinking together.

And he said he "missed her too," that he wished it was still summer and they could still be together, and that he continued to think about her a lot. He signed: "Love, Pete."

By the time his letter had reached Fort St. John, she had answered it, and her letter had reached their mailbox, it was already autumn on the calendar, later in September. She told him how thrilled she was to get the letter, how beautifully he wrote, and she asked how Mike was doing and if he thought he would be all right. She told him how happy she was to find that her English teacher this year was Mr. Trumbull, because he was a great Shakespeare teacher and she loved Shakespeare. She didn't mention Elinor again, but told him how she and some friends had thrown a surprise birthday party for her friend Chantal.

And she told him she still "missed him terribly" and thought about his "house in the trees" that she wished she'd seen in the daytime too, and how she felt she still hadn't totally returned home because her thoughts were still so much back there with him. And she signed: "Much love, and missing you, cutie, Dawn."

MEANWHILE, PETE, WHILE he kept longing for Dawn, couldn't help but notice a change that had occurred in him. He felt confident around girls. He knew it had to do with being with Dawn—and Laurie—in the summer. He didn't think it was such a big deal to talk to them anymore, that they were formidable or scary. And he noticed that they, too, now acted differently toward him.

In October Penny started glancing at him, asking him questions, pressing her hair back when he looked at her. One day, in study hall, she asked if he could help her with math. He said he wasn't too good in math either, but he could try. The teacher who was watching over the study hall told them they had to keep the noise down if they wanted to sit together and talk like that. They jointly made a mess of the math; he felt her arm touch his, saw her knee, heard her laugh.

The next morning, when people were still milling around in the hall before homeroom, he went right up to her and said: "Hey, Pen." He asked her if she wanted to go with him to Rick Capriano's party on Friday night, and of course, she said yes.

That night he couldn't sleep. *Three* girls?—three girls since July? And how could he—again—make Dawn part of a number? Yet he was doing it.

HE THOUGHT ABOUT whether to tell Dawn about Penny; then decided he had to.

It was still early October, and he still hadn't answered Dawn's last letter. He managed, finally, to write it simply and factually, as if it was no big deal. He signed it: "Love, Pete."

BY THE TIME HER next letter arrived it was well into October. He had already done things with Penny that the experiences with Dawn and Laurie wouldn't even have enabled him to imagine. Yet when he saw Dawn's letter in the mailbox, he felt a stab of pain.

She began—"Dearest Pete"—as if everything was still the same. She told him how impressed Mr. Trumbull had been with her paper on *The Winter's Tale* and how thrilled she was about his reaction. She told him she'd been applying to schools and her first choice was the University of British Columbia in Vancouver, that it was "not too close to her parents but not too far." She told him how it was already getting cold and how dazzling the yellow leaves were on her street. She told him how she, Elinor, and Chantal had gone to a slumber party at Vicki's house—and instead of slumbering had engaged in "silly girl talk" all night long.

At the end she wrote:

And about Penny! First of all, I want to thank you, dear Pete, for being so candid and telling me about it. I'm not surprised—I know that you're a sweet, decent person—but still I want to thank you for it. Now I cannot say that getting this news was the happiest moment of my life! But I knew you were surrounded by cute girls down there and that you yourself are irresistibly cute. I guess I was realistic—while, at the same time, trying not to be. There were things I wanted to say to you if we had been able to have that third meeting. But when I got back here, I thought about it more, and I said—why not be realistic. Anyway, I hope that you don't think that this in any way means that there is any less of a connection between you and me. Yes, there is a great geographic distance between us, and I guess it's a fact of life. But—for me—a profound connection is not dissipated by what it says on a map. Which means, I guess, that I hope that you will please continue to write to me, and tell me everything that's going on—and soon!

Much love,

Your eternal friend,

Dawn

# 6

In September the next year Dawn moved to Vancouver, where she'd been accepted at her first-choice college. She wrote to Pete soon after the move. She told him how nice her roommate seemed; how she had always liked Vancouver and was thrilled to find herself living in it; how, while she didn't exactly feel nostalgia for home, it was strange not to be there anymore after being there all her life.

Pete, while happy to get her letter as usual, wasn't having one of his best times. Penny was long gone; she'd started, while they were still together, flirting openly with Ray Alford; then, one evening, had called Pete and said: "We need to talk about our relationship." She was with Ray now.

Around that time Pete had found himself—while having made the varsity basketball team—strictly confined to the bench, the coach never even playing him for a minute or two; until finally he'd quit the team in disgust. That left him without a sport, since basketball had been his only sport. That night—a cold night in February—he went out walking in the Knolls with Mike, and they drank so much that when Pete got home he threw up.

Mike—now the only one of his friends who, like him, wasn't on any of the teams—was also in danger of being expelled from the school. Half the days he didn't come in at all, and his grades were near failing.

Pete told Mike—they were sitting, drinking, in Mike's living room, Mike's father out on a date—that maybe he should have tried to stay together with Dawn somehow, that he now felt she was the last good thing left in his life.

"Pete, my man," said Mike. "You told her all about Penny, right. She tell you about any guys?"

"She's not interested in the guys in her school. She told me that."

"Oh, yeah," said Mike.

He drank some of the whiskey in his glass, sighed.

"Not interested in any of them. Not in a single solitary one of them. And not interested in the guy at the corner drugstore either, right? And not interested in the guy at the hamburger joint, right? Nope, she's only got eyes for you, pal, three thousand miles away, on the other edge of the planet." He said: "Come on, Pete. Don't let her put one over on you. They're always putting one over on us."

Pete vaguely shook the whiskey at the bottom of his glass; stared glumly ahead of him.

As the fall progressed—Dawn continuing to write to him often—Pete began to feel abashed that she was a college student while he was still a high school kid.

His parents were getting on his case to start applying to schools, but he was only doing it listlessly. He thought it might be better to take next year off and just work—or something. He wasn't at all sure what he wanted to do.

"We're just cannon fodder for them," said Mike. "First they were shipping us off to Vietnam. Then, when enough guys starting coming home in boxes and enough parents were getting upset about it, they stopped doing that. Now you have to volunteer to go over there and come home in a box. It's all a big machine, Pete. They need us for their corporations. Sure, be a good student, go to college, get straight A's. You know how they treat my father now at GE? They treat him like crap. No pay raise in ten years. They pass him over for all the big projects. He's a slave there, Pete. You should hear him. He says it himself. Don't let them rope you in, Pete. Don't play their game."

In November Dawn wrote that there was a "really interesting" guy in her Victorian Poets class. But when she tried to get his attention, she said, it was so difficult that she wasn't sure if he liked girls.

Pete, for his part, was taking few courses now in twelfth grade. Sometimes, in the middle of the day, he'd leave school and walk through the woods till he came to his yard. The trees were mostly bare now, a few brown and gold leaves still fluttering. Charlie ran up happily to see him.

In December he wrote to her that he didn't think they should keep writing. He said they seemed to be going separate ways now. He said that when they met they were both kids, and she already wasn't such a kid. He said he had no way of getting to British Columbia, and he thought they would just keep getting more distant from each other. He said all his memories of her were fond ones.

And so he lost her.

# North-Country Girl

THERE SHE IS, the north-country girl—stepping out the door of the inn, coming down the path to greet me. The white fur lining of her hood—I can't quite see this yet, but can imagine it—pushes out her thick black hair in glossy bunches; her cheeks are red and her breath puffs before her in little exuberant mists; her body in the parka is endearingly supple and succinct. And beyond it—beyond the girl, the inn—the frozen lake.

Yes, she's come to greet me, as I knew she would; and the cool moist kiss holds promise of long nights under the quilt. But for now, she says, she doesn't think it would be a good idea for me to enter the inn. Her father is there, and he might not be prepared to see me yet. For now I should just get settled in one of the bungalows, the little separate ones out on the shore of the lake.

## 2

The inn—meaning this whole establishment—is closed in the winter. But the north-country girl and her father stay here—in the inn proper—the year round. And why shouldn't they, since it's a magnificent place—three-storied, soft-carpeted, warm, with a spacious dining hall, recreation rooms, sauna, even a bar with soft shadows and glinting bottles.

The north-country girl's father is from Canada, broad, burly, and silent. Over the years, the only obstacle to what would be our perfect happiness together.

She's seen to it that I'll be comfortable here in my bungalow. Admittedly, there's an aspect to it—of being, among the seven or eight bungalows here on the lip of the lake, in the only inhabited one, of feeling the emptiness of the others—that not even she could do anything to assuage. But the heat and hot water are working, the bed sheets and linen are fresh and fragrant; there's even, next to the fireplace—in case I'll want a homey touch—a neat pile of wood, and of course, in the cabinet, her simple and wholesome provisions of bread and doughnuts and things.

## 3

Three days have passed since I arrived. I'm still here, in the bungalow. It isn't bad here. I was working hard these last months; I appreciate the quiet, the chance to unwind a little.

The north-country girl has stopped in on me often. Well, not that often—and not at all, actually, since yesterday evening—but I understand the predicament she's in. The other days she brought me hot food from the kitchen; she was sweet and solicitous, asked if I was warm enough at night.

… Generous, yes, with the food; but … Sitting on the bed, and suggesting that she stay awhile, I couldn't seem to get anything from her but a confused evasiveness. I didn't mince words: I said I saw no reason why we had to wait until I finally moved into the inn—her room in the inn, where I always end up eventually and in which we've spent our sweet hours together—I said I saw no reason why we had to wait until that point until we … (and here I just gestured at the bed). Well, as I've said, she was in a difficult situation; it would have aroused suspicion if she'd stayed here much longer.

## 4

I decided to take a walk on the lake. In the years I've been staying here, I've never done it; and now it's very solidly frozen and the idea seems interesting.

Also, it will give me something to do. My lady of the inn, of course, continues to visit me—but less often lately, and the times between her visits have been getting kind of tedious.

So, one day, I start out. A clear February day like the ones we've been having lately, bright blue breaking through the grey that had veiled the sky and the lake since soon after my arrival—when was it? Way back in December. The lake is a white plain around me; the sharp air, the sun on my face, are exhilarating. I hear the sullen grind of my boots on the snow as I plod out—farther and farther out. Something seems to be pushing me, almost gleefully. Well, I might as well go with it.

After a while I can no longer see the American shore behind me, nor the Canadian shore ahead of me. I'd like to keep going till I can see the Canadian shore—maybe that's the goal toward which I'm being pushed. But how much farther is it? How wide is the lake here? In truth, despite all the years I've been coming here, I don't know. Meanwhile I find myself in kind of a pure, white place that could almost be the moon.

# 5

Now the air around me has turned bluish, the snow with a bluish tint, and I realize it must be dusk. I'm surprised—I wasn't aware that I've been out here quite this long, I guess I should turn back. The problem is I'm a bit disoriented; somewhere I lost the sense of which direction the shore is in—the Canadian shore; or the American shore for that matter. I could have gauged it by the sun, but I didn't think to, and now the sun is down.

I'm not worried; in the worst case, if I end up spending the night out here, I'm dressed warmly—a coat, boots, mittens. I didn't think to bring a scarf, but it probably won't get too windy. Maybe I should just keep walking, in one direction, and hope it's either north or south and eventually I'll get to one of the shores. If it's the Canadian shore, though, for all I know it's just wild country, won't help much.

I expect that, in any case, the north-country girl will be stopping by the bungalow; she hasn't been there in quite a while, and she's really overdue. She'll see I'm not there, and she should be able to make out the tracks leading to the lake, and out on the lake. Then she can get help, maybe a helicopter. I'll just have to wait out the night and see what happens.

# Leaving the House with Hani

THAT WAS THE hardest part—continuing to live together for a couple of months after we'd decided to end it. We were allowed to break the lease, but only if we gave two months' notice. Hani and I agreed that whoever found a new place first could be the first to leave.

I suppose it didn't help matters that it was autumn. That is, it was mid-September when we made our decision. Autumn in the northern-Jerusalem neighborhood where we were living isn't a matter of gold, scarlet, and orange leaves. Most of the trees are pines, and few of the deciduous ones change color; it's a more subtle matter of shortening days, growing shadows, white clouds that—after the endless hot heavy blue of summer—are like invaders from some strange country. Those clouds ... they give a shock of impermanence, they say all will dissolve in cold, rainy nights with stray cats huddled under cars.

No, it didn't help that we made our decision just as autumn was beginning, and then, as it progressed, had to keep inhabiting, like ghosts, the womb from which we'd exiled ourselves. We became formal and considerate toward each other; when she came home in the late afternoon, we'd exchange facts about the events of the day, show a polite interest in each other's lives. Meanwhile the nights grew cooler; the daytime maintained the façade of summer but the nights already belonged to a different season.

## 2

Nor did it help, I suppose, that the pool, which belonged to a nearby hotel and for which we'd both taken out memberships, stayed open till the end of October. Hani stopped going; she'd never liked it particularly, she'd gone there just to be with me. But I kept going—because the swimming was good exercise, because I liked the place, and because, I suppose, I didn't want to let at least my own expensive membership go to waste.

To friends back in South Bend, it sounds like a wonderful thing to have a pool stay open—and to have the weather stay amenable to swimming in it—till the end of October. It's like getting another, and another, and another extension on summer—endlessly, it seems. But to me, that year, it seemed like mockery. No, not mockery, exactly.

I'd come there on an October morning, a morning of soft gold, in time to see that moment when the sun, still vivid orange, surmounted a palm tree on the eastern side of the pool and cast a first flame over the water. There'd be just the lifeguard—hanging around, bored, nothing to do; an attendant or two; a handful of swimmers, mostly, like me, people with memberships, from the neighborhood. Almost an intimate atmosphere; no one talking, everyone knowing each other. An atmosphere, too—to me, at least—of aftermath; the days of summer, the crowds, the tourists, long passed; leaving only this gentle echo, this pleasant indolence. Except that there was such a lenience, a nonchalance, in it, that it seemed fate could almost just give a shrug and let it come back, let summer and all that, then, had still existed, come back.

No doubt they remembered me as the one who, in those days, was always there with that girl; the rather unlikely pair, the blond American with his heavy accent, the dark, petite home-grown girl in her turquoise swimsuit. But no one, now, ever said: "Where's your friend?"; they never asked about her. Perhaps they thought that, now it was autumn, she'd returned to some full-time schedule (in fact, she had—but that wasn't why she never came there); perhaps they were too delicate; or perhaps they just didn't care. But their non-asking created a sense of it being almost natural, inevitable, that she not be there anymore, enhanced the atmosphere of aftermath, acceptance.

Except that summer kept lingering in the sunlight; except that even as I swam my laps, leisurely, from one end of the pool to the other, melancholy would envelop me; except that as I sat, afterward, in a chair, it could—other than a few nuances, like the deep shadow that still covered most of the lawn—have been just a morning in summer, Hani and I arrived for an early swim before the crowds came.

# 3

One day in about mid-October, I heard Hani talking on the phone with someone she'd never, or not very much, talked with before; it was a man, and she had something special in her tone.

I wasn't having one of my best times. I'd written a sort of maudlin, pop-oriented book about my divorce; and I'd chosen to go to Israel to write it. Call it vestigial religiosity, my father having been a minister; I had an urge for flight, and it was just the first place that came up among the possible candidates. The idea, in any case, was to make some money with such a book, and then have more time for my real writing. I'd worked various jobs in my life—salesman, editor, waiter— and they'd all bored me to death. Writing was the only thing that, at least, wasn't boring.

I'd managed to get the book accepted by Chauncey, Steele in England; but now they were making trouble. They'd deferred its release date a half-year; a new guy had read it, and he'd decided it needed to be less bitter, more "edifying" or something like that. I still had money from the advance, but it was running out. Elinor (not her real name), back in South Bend, was getting clamorous about payments. I had only a few more weeks to find a new flat, but, considering my weak Hebrew and the fact that I wasn't employed in any normal way, my search hadn't been a picnic so far.

When Hani got off the phone there was still something special, altered, about her; her color, a sparkle in her eyes. Something communicative—irrepressibly; something that wanted to communicate, despite everything, with me, or with whoever would have been there.

"Who was that?" I said. I was sitting on the living room couch; Hani had been talking in the kitchen, and had just come into the living room.

"That?" she said. "No one you know."

We spoke in English; as I mentioned, I'd attained some Hebrew, but Hani was a grade-school English teacher, fairly proficient at it.

I said: "A man?"

"Yes."

"Someone you met recently?"

"Yes."

"You seem excited about it."

"I do? Oh …" She blushed.

"Want to tell me about it?"

All this time I'd been sitting on the couch, she standing in the middle of the room; now she came over and, tentatively, put one hand on the backrest of the couch, one knee on the cushion—at the other end, of course.

"Byron, do you want to know about this?"

"Yes," I said.

She looked at me—her dark, bright gaze.

"Are you sure?"

I, myself, didn't know why I was acting as I was—something in me was trying to stop me—but I said: "Sure, why not."

Now she settled onto the couch—the other end; we used to get quite close to each other on the couch. I could see both her dubiousness and her uncontainable communicativeness.

"Well," she said, "I met him at school."

"What, he's a teacher?"

"No. He's from the Education Ministry. He comes and gives lectures to the English teachers."

"Oh. So … you met him?"

"Yes."

"And you like him."

"Well, yes … I think so … He is single. He is thirty-four."

We both sat silent, as if that number had some special meaning. It did, actually; Hani was then about twenty-nine, I was forty-three. She always told me it didn't matter, but I never believed it.

"So," I said, "you going out on a date?"

"Not yet," she said. "He is supposed to call in a few days, to arrange one." She said: "Byron, you're not happy."

"I'm fine."

"Byron."

"I want us to be friends. I want us to be able to talk about things like this."

She said nothing. I picked up my iPad from the coffee-table in front of me and started looking at it.

She may have stayed there and tried to say something else, or she may have just drifted away—I don't remember.

DURING THAT PERIOD, when we were still living there but no longer together, I slept on the living-room couch, which was also a foldout bed. In addition to our old bedroom there was another room, but I used it for writing and didn't want to sleep there; I wanted to keep it "pure." I didn't mind letting Hani have the bedroom while I slept on the couch; it may have been chivalry, or that I've never cared much about things like that.

That night, though, at an hour when I would normally have been sleeping or trying to, I sat awake on the couch, a drink before me on the coffee table. It was pretty chilly out, but not enough, they judged, to turn the central heating on yet, so that it was kind of chilly in the room, too. It was dark—the shutter was mostly drawn, and I hadn't turned on a light.

At some point, Hani got up to go to the bathroom. This was unusual—she would generally sleep straight through the night.

After she flushed, turned off the light, and came out, I could just see her form in the hall from where I was sitting, and I said: "Hani."

She glided—a presence—to some point in the living room, and stopped.

"Byron?"

"Can we talk for a couple of minutes?"

She stood, uncertain.

"OK."

She came over, slowly, and sat in a chair to my left, against the window.

I said: "Couldn't sleep."

"No," she said. "I can see that."

I sank my forehead into my hand, sighed.

I said: "Hani, I'm thinking ... maybe the reason it didn't work out between us is that I'm not Jewish?"

She sat still; if she made some look, some gesture, of weariness, I couldn't pick it up through the dark.

She said: "Byron, you are always saying things like that." She said: "You are saying that it's because you're too old, it's because you're not Jewish. I've told you already, it's nothing like that. It's because of us, our personalities. We don't fit. We are not two people who fit together."

"And because I wouldn't make much of a father."

"Byron, oy."

Now she did sit back, sigh.

"I've talked to you about that. Do I have to talk about it again? OK, I will. I believe that you really want to be a father. I believe that you'd make a good one. You're a nice, warm person. It has nothing to do with that. It has nothing to do with these things that you torture yourself about. Byron, I don't know why you torture yourself like this."

"But maybe if I was Jewish, you wouldn't feel me to be so different."

"Oy, Byron. There are many Jewish people that I feel totally alien to. It has nothing to do with it. We are different people. We have different goals. I am a practical person, I am thinking about the here and now. You are a dreamer, you are thinking about ... the sunset, or whether there's God ... you know, you know what you are thinking about. Byron, I think the way you are is very good. I admire it. But it is not for me, I cannot live my life with a person who is like this."

She added—seeming to hesitate—"And I don't think you would be happy with someone like me. I don't think you would, in the long term."

I sipped my drink. I fell silent. For a long while, no one said anything. I sensed that she would rather be in her room, trying to get back to sleep; that she was staying there out of kindness. I had a feeling of appreciating it.

I said, finally: "Hani, do you ever think about us ... you know, doing it again, like we used to?"

She said, after a time: "Yes, I've thought about it."

"I guess ... I think it would be too strange."

She said: "Yes, I think it would be too strange, too."

"Something very deep in me would be too confused by it."

"Yes, you put things like that well. Something deep in me would be confused by it, too."

I said: "So, I guess we better get to sleep."

"Yes," she said. She stood up.

She said: "Good night, Byron."

"Good night."

She lingered a moment longer; she said: "Get some sleep."

"I'll try."

But probably, after she went back to her room, I kept drinking, and didn't get to sleep yet for quite a while.

## 4

Not long after that, though, I found a place. It was close by—in fact, in the same neighborhood. Perhaps that wasn't wise, psychologically speaking, but I didn't have a car, and hadn't particularly relished taking buses or taxis to look at flats that were farther away; I'd mostly looked at ones in the nearby area. In fact, this flat was in a building very near the hotel, the one where the pool was. This is, actually—two years later, I still live here—a quite beautiful stretch of street, with stone houses, apartment buildings of the same golden stone, palms and pines, hedges, bright flowers, all under the Mediterranean blue of the sky.

Naturally, I was happy, relieved, to have found the flat. But after signing a *zicaron devarim*, preliminary agreement, with the landlord, as I was walking back to the place where Hani and I still lived, I knew that my feelings wouldn't just be a matter of simple elation. I knew I would have to deal with a certain finality that was involved here. The lease started November 1—a week away; the landlord wasn't particularly concerned about my moving-in date, but there was no reason to put it off, was there?

It was late afternoon, and when I got back to our place, Hani had already come home before me. She was, these days, in a radiant mood; I knew it was because of Lior, with whom she'd had her first, apparently promising couple of dates. Not that I'd talked about it directly with her; but it was possible to infer what was happening from overhearing her phone conversations, from the general air about her.

She was in the kitchen as I came in, heating up water for coffee.

She came to the entrance to the kitchen.

"Hi," she said. "Want some coffee?"

"OK," I said. "I found a place."

"What?"

"I found a place."

"Really?"

"Yeah."

"That's great." The coffeepot whistled. "Just a minute."

She came out a minute later, holding two mugs of coffee. She had a short skirt on, showing her brown legs. She smiled at me. She handed me one of the coffees where I sat on the couch; she settled into the chair by the window.

"Byron. That's great. Where is it?"

"Rehov Eshkol."

"Rehov Esh*kol*?"

"Yeah. You know, down by the hotel."

"I know." You could see that she was both perplexed, and determined to be cheerful about this. "It's very close."

"Yeah, well … why not? I really like this neighborhood."

"How many rooms?"

"Two."

"*Two*?"

"Yeah. That's really all I need, isn't it? One for sleep, one for work."

"It is for November 1?"

"Yeah. That's just a week now."

We both fell silent.

I said: "What about you?"

"What?"

"Did you decide whether to keep looking?"

"Oh … Yes, I decided I'll stop for now. I am thinking I'll just stay here for the time being."

There was something in the air: it was our mutual awareness that this was because she'd started dating Lior, her future was uncertain, it might be pointless to move now after all. But—as if it were esoteric, or classified, material—we couldn't refer to this.

I said: "Think you'll be able to afford it by yourself?"

"Well." She smiled. "It won't be easy. But I think I can manage it."

Another thing that was in the air was that we'd continue to be near each other, physically; would see each other in the supermarket and the like. But we couldn't refer to that, either. I don't remember, from that point, what if anything we talked about, but I'm sure it just drifted away into small talk.


THAT NIGHT IT all, let's say, got the better of me, and I did something a little odd. I went to a bar downtown—that isn't the odd thing—and stayed there drinking beer till quite late. Not that I do that so often; but that night I needed some outlet.

It was about three o'clock by the time I left, took a taxi back to my neighborhood. I heard myself, though, tell the driver that my destination was "Rehov Eshkol." I told myself it must be because I wanted to see my new building, the building where my new apartment was.

Yet when the driver, on Eshkol Street, asked where to let me off, I found myself guiding him to the hotel.

It was a cool autumn night, starry, windless. There was a fragrance from the many blooms that, even in this late season, made such a show during the day. Before me the hotel stood like a giant lit-up castle.

I realized what I was doing, what my goal was, but I didn't believe it. I began to make my way, in the grass, around the side of the hotel. You may think that, in this country with its problems, things are well guarded, secure; don't think it. I knew enough by now to know that there was a good chance I could do what I was doing completely unnoticed.

I came to the grillwork fence that surrounded the pool.

It was a little higher than me, but by peering through an aperture, I could make out what seemed like a total, almost eerie calm in there.

I climbed over the fence.

The darkness, the desertedness, struck me with a deep desolation. There was a plastic tarpaulin over the water. I made my way over to the shallow end, where I always sat—where the two of us used to sit. I got down on the grass; and I sat there, in the dark, for I don't know how long.

# 5

My book did get published, the following spring, and even sold fairly well for a while, so that I've been able to live off the royalties. Meanwhile I've had the time to write not one but two novels. The feelers I've sent out, though, have been enough to make me realize that getting them published will be a lot harder than with the divorce book—close, perhaps, to a mission impossible. Chauncey, Steele wouldn't even contemplate it, though I'm sure they would have if the other one had been more of a hit. Meanwhile, as the memoir starts to fade from the scene, the money from the royalties is dwindling. I won't be able to continue like this too much longer; I'll have to find some other way to get by.

Even though I published it under a pseudonym and, of course, changed all the names, Elinor somehow found out about it and for a while was threatening to sue. I learned to delete her emails before looking at them.

Lior moved in with Hani at our old place, quite soon after I moved out. So, for a while, I had the lovely experience of occasionally seeing them around the neighborhood; not only that, but the tension, the fear, that any moment I might see them. Hani, I might add, is very affectionate in public, while you're in her good graces. Then—lo, divine mercy—they apparently moved to a different part of the city, because I stopped seeing them.

Myself, I haven't met any women since leaving Hani, and I haven't really tried to. It would be difficult, considering my situation, my foreignness; it would take a motivation I don't seem to have. But I knew, at the time, that after Elinor and Hani, I wouldn't have much spunk left.

So it's been a very quiet life—and now, with the funds running out, too quiet. Only lately I've been emailing with a wealthy cousin in Hong Kong, with whom I was quite friendly back in South Bend while we were small children, before his family whisked him off to Hong Kong. He says he'd be quite willing to give me work in his business—drafting memos, something like that. I'm not sure about the dignity of such an arrangement. On the other hand, the idea of the security is appealing. So is the idea of flight, of flight to somewhere even farther, much farther.

Meanwhile, you'll still see me, of an autumn morning, relaxing in a chair at the pool, peering through sunshades at my iPad propped on my knees. There's golden light on the water, the atmosphere is of indolence, nonchalance. *Do you remember?* a voice inside me asks. Yes, I remember; it's almost, still, here, in the gleam of the palm fronds, the warm air of morning.

# Help Me, Rhonda

## Part One

"WAS THAT YOU playing the piano?"

"Yes."

"Wow, Joni Mitchell."

"Yes, it was 'Morning Morgantown.'"

"I know. I love that song."

"Oh, really? Yeah, I love it too."

"You're a pianist?"

"Not really. I just play by ear."

"By *ear*?"

"Yes."

"You played that by *ear*?"

"Yes. It's not really that hard. The song isn't that hard."

"Amazing."

"Oh, thanks."

"You don't seem to believe in elevators."

"Nah. I don't have the patience to wait for it. It's easier to just walk down already."

"I'm Rhonda, by the way."

"Oh. Nice to meet you. Andy."

"Nice to meet you, Andy. I really didn't expect to meet another American here."

"No. An American in a *binyan meshutaf* in Be'er Sheva … it's not what you'd expect."

"I would ask what brought you here but you're not that into answering questions about yourself."

"Oh. There might be something to that. But it's all right. You can ask."

"OK. What brought you to live in a *binyan meshutaf* in Be'er Sheva?"

"Well, I had a girlfriend in Be'er Sheva. Not in this building, but in Be'er Sheva. And then, we weren't together anymore, but I stayed here."

"Oh. OK. And, if I can sneak in one more, what do you do?"

"I'm a translator. Freelance. That's why you see me here a lot. I work at home."

"Oh. A translator from ..."

"Hebrew to English."

"Hebrew to English. So. You must be in Israel a long time for your Hebrew to be that good."

"Yes, pretty long. About thirty years."

"Oh, a veteran. Sorry I snuck in yet another question."

"It's all right."

We were standing on the fourth or fifth landing of the stairs of the *binyan meshutaf*—apartment building. My apartment was on the seventh floor, out of eight. Hers was right around here—I'd seen her moving in yesterday, flustered, trying to direct the movers.

She was tall, though not as tall as me. Her hair was dull brown but very long and thick. Her eyes were big, blue, and had something both merry and watchful in them. She wore a white blouse with blue lace trim and a floral-print skirt. She seemed to be in the thirty-five to forty range.

I said: "So what brought you to a place like this?"

"A place like this. Let's see. I was living in Kibbutz Habika'a. Know where it is? It's in the Jordan Valley south of Kinneret.[1] And, I guess my life had hit a dead-end there. Do you know Ron Esman, at the university?"

---

1   The Sea of Galilee.

"Ron Esman. Yes, I've heard of him. Psychology, right?"

"Yes. Right. I have a background in psychology. So, I'm supposed to start working on a project with him. Research on … prenatal bonding."

"Prenatal bonding."

"Yup. Kids start bonding with their mothers before they're born. They start recognizing her voice and things. At least, that's the theory."

"Oh. OK. And how long are you in the country?"

"Well, not that long. Seven years. I'm not what you call someone who came here out of Zionism. While I was still in Philadelphia I met a guy, Nati, from Kibbutz Habika'a. So, on to Kibbutz Habika'a."

"Oh. OK. What were you doing in Philadelphia?"

"In Philadelphia … which is where I grew up—I had a little practice of my own as a psychologist."

"Oh. OK. Pretty good. And so … where's Nati in this."

"Nati … has not been in the picture for a few years. Didn't work out. But, I hung on at the kibbutz a few more years. You wouldn't believe it, but I worked in the plastics factory. 'Liaison with overseas customers.' Then I decided I wanted something closer to my field. Ha-ha! My Hebrew still wasn't good enough to be a shrink for Israelis. So I started reading ads, and I saw Professor Esman advertising for a research assistant."

"Oh. And he took you on from Kibbutz Habika'a?"

"Yeah. On condition I move to Be'er Sheva. He liked especially that I'm a native English speaker—good for the project."

"So how do you feel about moving to Be'er Sheva?"

"I feel good about leaving the kibbutz—it was long enough already. Be'er Sheva? OK. I mean, Tel Aviv would be better. But you have to pay a fortune to rent an apartment there, and who wants to pay a fortune. One more nosy question—are you renting? Don't answer if it's too nosy."

"In Israel that's not considered a nosy question. Yes, I'm renting. I'm one of the homeless."

"Homeless! Oh, boy. Homeless and 'Morning, Morgantown.' This is really kind of interesting. If you don't mind my saying. But, actually, you do."

"No, it's OK."

"Andy—that's your name, right?"

"Yeah."

"Phew. For a minute I thought I'd confused you with someone. Andy, it's really interesting to talk with you in the stairwell here, but I have to run along. It would be nice to talk again. But, of course, we don't have to. I do *not* want to disrupt your translating and your piano playing, and I'm saying that for real."

"No, we should, we should talk more."

# 2

"It's not fancy. It's the landlord's furniture. I haven't tried to fix the place up."

"Not fancy. If you don't mind my saying, that's an understatement. Ha-ha! But I don't see a piano."

"No, it's in the bedroom."

"Oh. I hope you don't mind my asking, but if you could play something for me, that would be great."

"Not tonight. I don't play on Shabbat."

"Oh. I didn't think you were religious."

"I'm not. I just like the quiet of Shabbat. Also don't want to disturb people."

"Oh. OK. Yes it is really, really quiet here, isn't it?"

It was early June, and there was still some dusk light. At the end of our talk in the stairwell, which was in the middle of the week, I'd invited her to come at this hour of Friday evening, mumbling—so that it wouldn't be an issue—something about it being after supper. I'd realized that, with her apartment still in disarray, I should be the one to invite. Also, I didn't want to ask her to go with me somewhere in the city; I thought this could be a way of avoiding that.

She'd come very promptly; I'd said "around eight-thirty" and she'd knocked diffidently on the door a very short time after that. She was wearing black pants and a saffron blouse with tiny sleeves that just barely encased her shoulders. Her face looked fresher, her hair both thicker and more orderly. There was a faint perfume smell.

She was sitting now in a chair across the coffee table, a chair I'd set up for her. I was on the couch. To my right, the sliding door was open on the small balcony. The buildings of the city stood very still in the late dusk.

I said: "Can I get you something to drink?"

She said: "Hm. That sounds nice. What have you got?"

"Well … orange juice. Sprite. Wine."

"*Wine*. That does sound tempting."

"I've got a good Cabernet from the Golan."

"Mmm, that sounds good. I am *not* a connoisseur. But I like Cabernet, at least I know that."

I got up from the couch, feeling very self-conscious. It had to do with my role as host, with which I've never been comfortable. But it also seemed to have to do with the great stillness in the apartment.

I went down the short, dark corridor, my bedroom on the left. I turned on the light in the kitchen. It looked terribly drab, and none too clean. Why hadn't I tidied it up a bit? I hoped she wouldn't come in here. I couldn't see any reason she would.

I took the bottle down from a cabinet, opened it with a corkscrew, poured two wineglasses to less than half full. I didn't want to put a lot of wine in either glass.

When I came back to the living room she was standing on the balcony, gazing out through the green grid that was fastened to the bars to keep out birds. I saw her from behind. She turned, saw the two wineglasses, and smiled.

"Thank you, sir," she said.

"Don't mention it."

I settled back onto the couch; she came in and settled back into her chair. Seeing her wineglass before her on the coffee table, she picked it up with long, delicate fingers.

"Mm," she said after a sip. "That gets the thumbs-up from me. But do not quote it in the wine journal."

I smiled. "It's all right, I don't write for them too often."

"I've *almost* never been in Be'er Sheva until this week." She was again looking toward the balcony, toward the night—almost night— sky. "I didn't know it has such an atmosphere. I mean, it's like, it replaces the desert, but at night the desert comes back."

"Yes. That's definitely what it's like." I said: "So, you met with Professor Esman?"

"Yeah. Yeah. Turns out he's really old. Did you know that? I didn't know that. He's a grandpa."

"No, I didn't know that."

"The campus is beautiful. I didn't know that either, that the campus here is so beautiful."

"Yes, it is." I thought to say: "I used to go there sometimes in the morning to write," but didn't say it. I said: "So how does he seem?"

"Uh … OK. He seems OK. I'm going to be reading a lot of literature on prenatal bonding. In the end I'm going to go back to the womb. Ha-ha!"

She sipped her wine, blushed.

"You have to sort of collate it for him?"

"Sort of. First I have to read a lot of *his* literature, from the voluminous mountains of stuff that *he's* published on this great subject. Then I have to read everything everybody else has ever written about it. Not really—that would take so many years I'd be as old as he is by the time I finished. I really don't know why I did this—becoming a research assistant at my age."

I thought: "Which is …?" but didn't say it. I said: "You said you weren't in Israel out of some kind of Zionistic reasons?"

"Zionistic reasons. No. No. I can't say that."

"So—just wondering—you said the thing with that guy at the kibbutz ended. Just wondering, then, why you wouldn't have gone back, if you had—it sounds like—a good setup in Philadelphia. You said you had a practice as a psychologist."

She sighed, sat back, made a nervous motion of smoothing her hair back on both sides.

"That," she said, "is a good question."

She kept sitting there, seeming to ponder a spot on the table.

She said: "Andy, wine loosens me up. Not only that, but you're a person one can tell things to." She said: "I kept staying at the kibbutz after Nati because I got involved with another man there. The really incredible thing is that it was a guy who was married. There I was, biological clock ticking blah blah … and I get involved with something totally hopeless and irrational. Oh, God."

She sighed, rubbed her eyes with both hands.

"So that's come to an end, too?"

She was still sitting with her hands over her eyes. She removed them, and gave me a complex, intensely lit gaze.

"Come to an end. Yes."

She sat forward again, picked up the wineglass—delicate fingers clasping the stem—and jostled the wine a little; but not the way a connoisseur does it, it was more of an absent motion.

"His wife found out, blah blah. They still seem to be together, thank God. They and their four kids. It's amazing, these secular kibbutzniks have loads of kids." She said: "So, by that time I was seven years in the country. My practice back home didn't exist anymore, I'd have had to reinvent it. I don't know. Maybe I just didn't have the energy to make another new start. Going back would have been like emigrating again. It was easier to just stay already. I don't know."

Her gaze had come to rest on me.

"And you," she said, "are getting away with not disclosing anything. Andy Lesser. I know *that* at least because I saw it on your mailbox."

"Great sleuthing work there. You've got a last name too, I take it?"

"Yes. And it's the same as it always has been. Greenspan."

"Rhonda Greenspan. Nice name, at least."

She gave me a bright, alert look; then broke into a small but intense, uncontrollable laugh. "I like the way you do that. The 'at least' is almost a dig. But then you balanced it with a compliment. Oh, God." She said: "Whatever I do, you know, you keep winning. I end up disclosing, and you don't disclose anything. But now, Mr. Lesser, we're going to put a stop to it. So. Had a girlfriend in Be'er Sheva. And what about before that."

"Before that Tel Aviv."

"And what were you doing in Tel Aviv?"

"Same stuff. Translating."

"That's not what I mean, sir. If you were a client I'd let you get away with this—for a while. But you're not a client. What about, you know, your personal situation in Tel Aviv?"

"In Tel Aviv I was divorced, just like I am now."

"OK. We're making slow, tortuous progress. And how long have you been divorced, sir?"

"Twenty years."

"Ah. OK. And you made *aliyah* thirty years ago, so this was well after your *aliyah*. So was this the person you moved to Israel with way back then?"

"Yes."

"And where is she now, if I may ask?"

"Tel Aviv."

"Aha. Kids?"

"Yes, two. I'm a grandpa."

Now she sat stock-still, looking at me.

"A grandpa."

"Yes."

"You, a grandpa."

"Yes."

"OK. I didn't have you pegged as a trickster, but now I think I'm seeing something else. The trickster rises to the surface."

"Nope, not a trickster."

She sat still.

"How old are you?"

"Fifty-three."

She kept sitting still.

"Fifty-three."

"Yes."

"*You* are fifty-three?"

"Yes."

She said: "Amazing. Amazing. You don't look fifty-three. God, I thought you were a little older than me." She said: "OK. Now wait a minute. Fifty-three and a grandpa. That's what you're telling me?"

Now she was looking at me shrewdly, as if, after all, I'd been pulling her leg all this time, but she was on to it.

I said: "And it's my younger kid who has the kid."

She sighed. "OK. You had kids when you were a kid? Your wife was a teenage mom?"

I laughed. "My son—the one who has the kid—is twenty-seven. He got married not long ago. My grandson is a year old."

She was still looking at me as if through a mist, as if too much was being asked of her.

"And your other kid?—the older one, I take it."

"Yes, the older one is my daughter. She's twenty-nine."

"She's twenty-nine. You're fifty-three. You got married young."

"Yes."

Her expression was if still sizing me up, still wary.

"And what do these kids do?"

"My son is a high-tech whiz in Tel Aviv. My daughter is in Iceland."

"In Iceland."

"Yes."

"In Iceland."

"Yes."

She sighed.

She said: "I feel as if I might be encroaching on a bit of an icy territory here."

I said: "Yes, there might be something to that."

She sighed again.

"I also feel as if I may be overstaying my stay."

"No, it's fine."

She looked at me.

"Andy, I know that you're not *mea ahuz* about my being here. And that you weren't totally pleased about inviting me, either. I don't know why. And frankly it's none of my business. And I should go."

"Rhonda, it's fine. Really."

She looked at me with her lips in a firm line, pushed hair back from her right shoulder. It had an effect; I wasn't sure if she intended it.

She said: "That, by the way, is the first time you've called me by my name."

"Well, I like the name."

She said: "OK. I know that when I asked what there was to drink, you gave a list of three things, and wine was the last of them. But. If I'm going to stay here, I have to have more of this wine. I *really* like it. And … it calms me down."

"OK. Fine."

We both glanced at her glass. It was empty; mine still had some wine in it.

I picked up my glass, drained what was left.

"I'll get a refill for both of us."

# 3

This time when I came back, holding the two wineglasses, she was again standing on the balcony; but when I set them on the coffee table and sat down on the couch, she didn't join me but kept standing there.

I looked uncertainly toward the right, where she was.

She said: "Nice night."

"Yeah."

I got up; I went and stood parallel to her, not too close.

It was already deep night, the stars bright. A half-moon was up, climbing near the wall of a building, incredibly bright. The buildings—tall but not skyscrapers, the tallest maybe twenty stories—looked very black and somber, here and there a gleam from a window.

She said: "'Night in the City.'"

I said: "I love that song."

She was a dark, still presence a couple of yards to my left; out here, in the pure, cool air, the perfume smell was stronger.

"Do you play it?"

"No. I mean I can, it's not hard. But it's impossible to play."

"Why is 'Morning, Morgantown' possible to play but not 'Night in the City'?"

"Because there's something in 'Night in the City' that you can't get on a piano. I mean, a better pianist could. Not that I've heard anyone try. Even on YouTube there's no piano cover, or attempted piano cover, of 'Night in the City.'"

She said: "Joni Mitchell was really something in those years."

"Joni Mitchell was phenomenal in those years. She was the best songwriter of that period, which is saying a lot. Her ten best songs were better than Lennon and McCartney's ten best songs. Some of her songs have chord changes that you've never heard anywhere, anywhere else in your life."

"Which ones do you play aside from 'Morning, Morgantown'?"

"Well, play—as opposed to just futilely fool around with—I can sort of make a go of 'Urge for Going,' 'Both Sides Now,' 'Michael from Mountains.'"

"I would love to hear you play 'Michael from Mountains.'"

"Well, it could be arranged."

"Yeah, if I push you into it."

"Well, I'm not sure you should put it that way."

"No, you're not sure. Ha-ha!" She said: "What's your background with music?"

"My background. Well, I'm from a musical family. My sister is a classical violist. Our parents played classical records all the time, and we both got to love it. But I took piano lessons for a couple of weeks when I was seven, about when my sister was starting the viola, and I couldn't stand it. Found it unbearably tedious. I quit after two weeks."

"That's your musical background?"

"When I was a teenager I got into the music everyone was into, and I found my way to the really beautiful stuff, like Joni Mitchell and James Taylor. Eventually I got into blues, and then jazz a lot, too. I listen to all of it now, classical, pop, jazz, I don't know, everything. I love some of the Israeli songs, too."

"But when did you start to play the piano, sir?"

"I started to play the piano when I was seventeen. Actually I started with blues, playing along with a record, a record that had a blues pianist on it. Eventually I started playing pretty songs that I liked, too."

"Just like that?"

"Well, I put quite a lot of time into it."

"But just like that? By ear?"

"Yes. All by ear."

"Can you read music?"

"No, not at all."

"Wow." She said: "Where, may I ask, did all this happen? Where did you, uh, grow up, and hear music, and start playing the piano, et cetera et cetera et cetera."

"It was in upstate New York. A place called Carrenden Park. A pretty rural area, between Albany and Schenectady, not that 'Schenectady' means anything to people either."

"Oh, I've heard of Schenectady."

"Yeah?"

"Yeah."

She looked out into the night. I did too.

She said: "Should we go a little religious, Andy?" She said: "I don't know what the hell I'm doing—I'm sure you can see that. You, if you don't mind my saying, said that you were 'homeless.' And we come upon each other here. What do you think? It just happens by chance?"

I said: "Well. I'm not sure. It's not easy to get me to see some kind of guiding hand, if that's what you mean."

She seemed to take this in silently.

She said, after a while: "Our wine is aging in solitude in there."

"Yeah, it is. We should keep it company."

# 4

"I think that when we were in here," she said, pulling up her chair, moving hair away from her face, picking up her glass, sipping delicately, "we left off with Iceland. With your daughter in Iceland."

"Yes."

She gave me a plain, blue-eyed gaze.

"What, may I ask, is your daughter doing in Iceland?"

"She met an Icelandic guy in Tel Aviv. He was here, I don't know, to do some work with an Israeli high-tech firm. She got involved with him, and she went back to Iceland with him." I said: "They're not together anymore. But she's still there. Working as a translator. She's kind of a language whiz, and she learned Icelandic very fast, so she's translating from Icelandic to English. She knows English too because we spoke it in the house."

"Aha," she said, with a kind of sparkle in her gaze that was really quite heart-capturing. "Like father like daughter."

"Yes, sort of."

She looked as if she wanted to say more, but thought better of it.

She said: "And the son in Tel Aviv?"

"Also kind of a whiz. High tech. He works for a famous cyber security firm, Migun, you've probably heard of them. Software developer."

"Mm," she said. "Lots of whizzes in the family."

I smiled. "Oh, I don't know."

"Is your ex-wife a whiz?"

"No. Intelligent, but not a whiz."

"Is she remarried?"

"No."

She said: "What's your grandson named?"

"My grandson?"

"Mm-hm. I know I haven't got the son's or the daughter's name from you, but I thought at least you could surrender the grandson's name."

"Oh. OK. I surrender. His name's Ori."

She was looking at me—looking quite beautiful.

"When you said that, Andy, you had a real smile. A real smile. The first time I've seen it."

"Oh. Well, he's quite a little guy."

She kept sitting there, with that look; I couldn't look back at her.

Just then her iPhone started buzzing in her pocket. She took it out, looked at the screen and frowned.

"Hello? … *Nimrod, ma shlomcha … Ani lo yechola ledaber achshav … Ani im anashim …*"[2]

She switched into English. "It's nice … Yeah. On Tuesday … Just some people who live here who invited me … Nimrod. *Can't* we talk later?"

She sat way back and sighed, parked one shoe on the edge of the coffee table. She looked drawn into herself, defensive. She shot me a look of glum exasperation.

"Nimrod. *Nimrod* … This doesn't lead anywhere … No … Nimrod, you were fine before we started our thing. You were fine … Of course I take responsibility. Of course I—Nimrod. I can't undo what was done … Nimrod, this doesn't lead anywhere for you. The only way for … The only way for you is with Ariela. She's a great woman … You want to tear everything down now? Go ahead. No one's going to stop you, Nimrod. *Nimrod*. No one's going to stop you … No because it doesn't lead anywhere, it just makes things worse. No. Nimrod—I didn't say never. I didn't say never. You want to meet in a café in a few years, if everything's quiet, if everything's OK again, I'd be glad to … OK maybe less than a few years. I don't know. I'm not sitting here with a stopwatch … I didn't say—I didn't say I was *beseder* …[3] Because I knew when to stop. I knew when it was—" She said: "Damn"—looking in a harried way at the iPhone screen.

She set the iPhone—the screen now mute—on the coffee table. She sat forward again, buried her face in her hands.

---

2  "Nimrod, how you doing … I can't talk now … I'm with people …"

3  "OK" or "all right," meaning her behavior.

A dog barked, lengthily and as if astonished by something. Another, more distant dog barked, as if surprised and outraged.

I said, "That's the married guy?"

When her face came out from her fingers, I saw glumness and pain there I hadn't seen before.

"Yeah. He's having some kind of regression because I left. Left the place."

"He wants to meet with you?"

She made a scornful motion with her hand.

She was gazing off into a space of her own, yet she talked to me. "Andy, why I did such a thing, I still don't know. I guess—I guess—I just felt stranded. The thing ended with Nati, and there I was, alone in this kibbutz, with all these families, and I was this solitary being ..." She said: "Nimrod is CEO of the plastics factory. He's quite a person. He's a reserve major in Tzahal.[4] He's been in wars, he's got scars and a bullet lodged permanently in his back. We were just ... he was there every day when I came in to work. Maybe I was just reaching out to some daddy. I don't know ..." She said: "Or maybe it was revenge."

"Revenge for what?"

"Revenge at the world, for the way I'd ended up, for the way I was just stranded while other people had these lives, these families, these purposes ..." She said: "I know, I should have left the kibbutz then. Back to America, somewhere else in Israel, but just left the kibbutz. I wasn't exactly beloved among all the married women there. Especially after it ended with Nati. But ... Nimrod was there at work every day. I couldn't leave Nimrod. Couldn't."

She sat silent, looking into her space.

She moved her gaze to me. It was almost a mechanical motion, her eyes still, almost expressionless.

She said: "So who is she, Andy, this woman in Be'er Sheva?"

I moved on the couch. I leaned over, took a sip of my wine, put the glass down delicately.

---

4   The Hebrew acronym for the IDF, the Israel Defense Forces.

"Her name's Hila."

"When did you break up?"

"It was a little over a year ago." I said: "We were together quite a long time, actually. Eight or nine years. It started when I was still in Tel Aviv. We'd get together on weekends. Then we decided—I was having trouble paying my rent in Tel Aviv, not that that was all of it, but it was part of it—we decided that I should move here, to Be'er Sheva. Not that we should live together, but close to each other. She's got a couple of daughters. Also a huge dog I can't stand."

She was—in a quiet way—very riveted on what I was saying.

"It ended?"

"Yeah …" I said: "It was kind of a shock to me. My road has been pretty rocky. I thought this, at last, was something that would last. I didn't … I didn't think it would end."

We both sat in the silence.

She said: "She still lives close to here?"

"Yeah."

"Do you see her?"

"Almost never."

She said: "So. You still seem to be in it."

"'In it.' Yes, you could say." I said: "Rhonda, I'm a retiree from life."

"Retiree?"

"Yeah."

"You're fifty-three."

"I know. There are still New York State workers retiring at fifty-five."

She kept looking at me, and I knew that the line between a conversation of friends and a therapy session was now very thin. But I also knew that I'd drunk wine and would keep talking.

I said: "I was a writer. I've written some novels over the years … I'd try to get them published, and not succeed, and then I myself would no longer approve of them and put them away … Finally a couple of years ago an agent in New York reacted to one of them. He said it had 'real potential,' but I had to make some changes. So of course I made them. It was a matter of two chapters that he wanted to be changed around, pretty substantially. I worked months on it—wanted to get it exactly right. Then I sent it to him again ... So I waited and he didn't answer. After a few weeks I emailed him. After a couple more days he sent me an email saying he still wasn't convinced the novel was 'viable in today's tough market.'"

We sat in the silence.

She said: "Andy, do you know anyone in Be'er Sheva?"

I mulled this, as if there were something complicated about it.

"No ... Hila used to say that too. Why don't I join some club or other? I don't know. The motivation doesn't reach the line on the scale." I said: "Now, as a retiree, I'm even less motivated." I said: "This business with the novel and the agent weighed me down. I turned pretty gloomy. Not only that, but impatient with Hila. She's from an old pioneering family. It's a practical ethos. You wake up in the morning, you see a problem, you solve it. You don't mope. It's not a bad way to be. But if you're moping, and someone looks down on the moping, it can create something that keeps getting worse. She didn't understand why I stopped trying to publish the book and stopped writing. She didn't realize how much of a blow it was with the agent. I got irritable with her—and *davka*[5] she was very sensitive and vulnerable to that. She started saying: '*Ata yodayah ma? Ani lo tsricha et ze.*'[6] I thought it was rhetoric. But she meant it."

I raised my hands and dropped them.

"It's enough, Rhonda. I live a quiet life as a translator. I've got Yishai, Maayan, and Ori. Maayan is really nice, too—she sends me videos of Ori on WhatsApp. I'm not a satellite of them. I visit them about once in two weeks, and sometimes they come here. I don't move back to Tel Aviv—I guess because it's too expensive and also I might become a satellite. Here I can pay a low rent and not have to do as much work and not have the stress."

She said: "And live near Hila."

I sat still.

---

5 "Ironically."

6 "You know what? I don't need this."

I said: "It's not the reason, Rhonda."

"You've got memories of her all around you."

"Yes, and actually it's not an easy thing." I said: "When it ended with Hila, Ori was on the way. He was coming in a few months. I knew that, of course. It kept me going. Without that ... I'm not sure I would have kept going."

She said, finally: "Not sure you would have kept going?"

"No."

"What does that mean?"

"It means I might have ended it."

She sighed.

"And you think you can continue like this?"

"Yes. It's a bit Buddhist. No expectations, nothing to lose." I said: "Love and work, the cornerstones of human life—isn't that what Freud said? You can't imagine what it's like, Rhonda. No more 'Will I be loved? Will I get published?' Just quiet. Just the same, regular things every day." I said: "And a little piano playing in the evening."

She was sitting back, her arms folded, staring down and to the side.

She reached her foot out and put it against mine.

We sat there, our shoes pressing against each other.

The Shabbat evening seemed finally to reach an ultimate stillness. Everything was in it.

I said: "Rhonda, if it was simple."

We sat there in the stillness.

She said: "Yeah, and with someone like me it's not. At all. Right?"

I said nothing.

She moved her foot away.

She picked up her iPhone again and glanced at it.

She sighed.

"Ten-thirty. I should go."

"You don't need to."

She kept sitting there.

She said: "Why would I think anything good might be coming my way, after all the pain I've caused."

I said: "I don't think you should look at it that way."

She dropped her hands on her knees. She sighed again. She stood up, laboriously.

I did, too—also as if it were a big project.

I followed her through the living room to the tiny foyer and the door.

At the door she turned around and gave me a complex look that was tinged with irony.

She said: "Well, thanks."

I said: "Sure." I said: "I guess we'll be seeing each other around."

"Yes."

I said: "Weird situation, isn't it?"

She said: "Yes. Very weird."

She summoned a kind of smile. "Good night, Andy."

"Good night."

Going back to the coffee table, I saw the wineglasses. Mine still had wine in it, hers was empty.

## Part Two

I stepped out of the building. It was a late-September afternoon on Ben-Zvi Street, in the heart of Be'er Sheva. The stupefying heat of the desert summer had been replaced by gentle, golden light.

I was elated. I had just had a root canal, my first ever. A couple of months earlier a tooth—one that a large old filling could no longer support—had cracked; the dentist had told me that, before he could refurbish the tooth, it had to have a root canal. I'd made an appointment with the root-canal specialist he'd referred me to—and spent two months with a constant undercurrent of anxiety, which came to the surface at night. People had told me they'd had them and it hadn't been bad. But the words "root canal"—*tipul shoresh* in Hebrew—caused me anxiety I couldn't control.

Now I was elated because—with a nerve block and two doses of lidocaine—the whole thing had taken half an hour and hadn't involved the slightest twinge of pain. I'd actually enjoyed glimpsing the procession of incredibly refined instruments the specialist had used, marveling at the sophistication of it. With him hovering from the right, his young female assistant from the left, the two of them had kept up an animated, irrelevant chat throughout the procedure. I couldn't focus on it, but it didn't worry me; I realized that what he was doing was utterly routine to him, and he was obviously a master.

Now I stood on the sidewalk. People flowed by—Bedouin women in black veils and kerchiefs, soldiers, pensioners, tanned teenage girls in short shirts and clingy shorts—the usual mix. I realized that something in me was declining to go home; there was another idea. What was it? To go to a café. Of course. I wasn't supposed to eat for a couple of hours, but I could drink—drink an ice coffee, browse the latest news on my iPhone. Clearly this experience, with the tremendous relief I felt, was something to celebrate.

AT A PLACE where Ben-Zvi turned off into a pedestrian plaza, there was a café I liked—small, with some of its tables outside under an awning. As I approached, a woman had made her way from the other direction, from within the plaza, and was closer to the door than I was. I think, in retrospect, that I did recognize her, but something blocked the recognition. She was tall, quite lithe and shapely in jeans and a frilly, pale blue top that didn't make it to the jeans, giving glimpses of pale, soft skin.

Finally, recognition rose to consciousness.

I said: "Rhonda!"

She stopped, one hand on the door handle, and turned to look at me.

"*Andy!*

"Fancy meeting you here."

"Yes. Another of our mystical encounters."

"Mystical … wow."

She said: "Going in?"

"Yeah. Would you want to sit at a table outside here?"

Her eyes did a reconnaissance of the tables.

"Yeah, sure. I think we have to order inside first."

"Yes, we do."

Pushing open the door, she flashed a smile over her shoulder at me. The combination—the smile, the jeans, the pale skin—made me feel queasy.

Inside, after she heard me order only an ice coffee, she said: "Aren't you going to eat anything?"

"I just got out of a root canal."

"A *root canal!*" she said, with a look of dumbfounded horror.

SINCE THE TIME she'd visited me on a Shabbat evening about three and a half months back, I'd hardly talked with her. Now and then our paths crossed in the stairwell and we did little more than greet each other. It was in one of those instances—it was very soon after the Shabbat-eve visit—that I'd said: "You should stop by again."

She'd stood and looked at me for a few moments.

She'd said: "Andy, it's nice of you to offer. I don't think it's the right thing for me now. It's nice that you see me as someone to chat with. I think I … I think I'd see it as a little more than that. I don't think it would be good for me now."

I'd looked at her, with many contending voices within. But I'd said: "All right. The offer stands, though."

She'd flickered me a smile. "Thanks."

NOW I SAT down at the last table in the row, in cool and lovely late-September shade. The table looked out toward the train station. Between Ben-Zvi and the train station, too, the city's enterprising mayor had had a plaza built, this one so thick with walled-off squares of trees that you had to wend your way through it.

Sitting down behind her tray, which bore a cappuccino and an almond croissant, she gave me an intense, quizzical look.

"A *root canal!*"

"Yeah. A tooth cracked two months ago. I've been living in anxiety for two months."

"Oh God. Please don't tell me about it. It's causing me anxiety … God."

"But what I have to say is reassuring."

"Reassuring?"

"Turned out it didn't hurt at all."

She gave me a blue, round gaze.

"He just gave me the anesthetic and … totally painless."

"Oh. Well, I wish I could say I was reassured because a friend of mine had a root canal and she said it was *awful*."

"Oh. Don't tell me about *that*."

She sipped her cappuccino.

She said: "We don't really talk. And now they're forcing us to."

"Yeah, 'they.' Whoever they are."

She looked at me silently a few more moments. She seemed to be thinking deeply.

"So how have you been doing? Aside from root canals."

"Well … OK. Same stuff, I guess. Doing a literary translation for a change."

"Mm. Literary?"

"Yeah. Mostly I've translated political stuff. The first ten years or so that we lived here, we lived near Jerusalem and I had a job as editor. It was for a world-politics institute at Hebrew University. So when I became a freelancer, my contacts were in that field, with political think tanks, and that's who I translate for. Now one of the profs who's a client asked if I could translate a memoir by his wife, about her girlhood in Iraq. It's really good. It's on a literary level."

"And your own writing?"

"My own writing?" I raised my hands and dropped them. "I'm a retiree."

"Yeah, don't we know it."

I gave an uncertain laugh.

"However," I said, "my daughter has returned from Iceland."

"Oh?"

"Yeah. I guess she'd had enough. She's back in Tel Aviv."

"Oh. So there's hope for retirees."

I said: "Yeah. Maybe there is." I said: "So what have you been up to?"

She completed a sip from her cappuccino, and—a bit elaborately—cleared her throat and set the mug down.

"I ... have been up to pretty amazing things."

"Oh, yeah?"

She said: "In a week and a half I'm moving to Canberra."

"Canberra."

"Mm-hm."

"*Canberra.*"

"Yup."

"That's Australia."

"Yup."

"What the hell happened?"

"Well," she said—her eyes rising to mine in a very soft, complex way, "I met a guy."

I sat gazing at her.

"Professor Esman?"

She burst out laughing. She pushed her chair back and laughed uncontrollably into both hands. When her face finally emerged, there was a tear down the left side of it.

"Oh, God," she said. She wiped at the tear. "Andy, you are really something. You come up with humor at a time like this." She said: "No, not Professor Esman. He's quite a bit younger. His name's Denny Holcomb. He's an *oleh*[7] from Australia. But he wants to go back."

"How'd you meet him?"

"Well. He's a shrink like me. He also did work once for Professor Esman, and he had to help me with something. So ... we met."

"What, he's here in Be'er Sheva?"

"Mm-hm. He had a clinic here. Still does, actually. But not for much longer."

"Why don't I ever see this guy?"

"Because I go to his place. It's nicer."

"So is he—I hope you don't mind my asking—"

---

7 "Immigrant."

"No, go ahead—"

"Divorced?"

"Mm-mm."

"Single?"

"Mm-hm."

"Hm. Well. How long's he been here?"

"In Israel?"

"Yeah."

"Nine years."

"And he wants to go back?"

"Yup."

"Why?"

"Why." Her eyes strayed off to her right—toward the clumps of trees, the train station. "Why."

She returned her gaze to me. She looked at me for some moments.

She said: "Andy, I can't believe it, but I'm doing this again. Telling you things. Because of this feeling that you're someone one can tell things to."

"Well," I said, "it's a compliment, Rhonda. Thanks."

"He wants to go back," she said, "because, he says, he doesn't really feel at home here. His Hebrew's good. He's got good work. But … he says it's taken him this long to realize that Canberra—Canberra specifically, Australia in general—is his real home."

I looked at her. "You're not crazy about this."

"No. I suppose not. I suppose I'd be happier if we could stay here."

"You were saying, that other time we talked, that you're not a big Zionist."

"I know … I said a lot of things that night, in a state of confusion." She said: "Andy, I've gotten sort of attached to this place. I don't know. People are more like me here. More open. More brazen you might say. Am I making sense?"

"Yes, of course. You do kind of fit in here."

"It's not only that. It's … Jewish stuff from my childhood."

"What kind of Jewish background did you have?"

She sighed.

"*That* is a story ... My father was a lapsed Orthodox Jew. Chaim Greenspan. Lapsed, but there was still a lot of religiosity about him. I wouldn't say that—the fact that he had that tendency, while my mother was quite secular—was the reason they divorced when I was ten. But it had something to do with it."

"Did he try to make you religious?"

"No. I think that was sort of an understanding—a fragile understanding that they had—that he wouldn't do that with me and my sister. He'd stopped going to synagogue himself, but he'd do a Kiddush ceremony on Friday evening. I found it kind of beautiful. His piety was always there, it was part of him, it was a presence, even when he didn't express it in any way. And he cared about Israel a lot. He was always following what happened with Israel. And he didn't say 'the Israelis,' he said 'the Jews.' 'The Jews' this, 'the Jews' that ...'"

I said: "He's in the past tense?"

She was sitting very still, looking at a point on the table.

"There was so much we didn't talk about that other time ..."

"No. It wasn't very long."

She said: "He died when I was fourteen. After the divorce I didn't see him that much. The divorce wasn't on such good terms. He moved to Harrisburg, which is not that far from where we lived in Philadelphia, but I didn't see him much. And then—" She raised her hands and dropped them. "He had a heart attack and died. He was fifty-one. He smoked, but not all that much—at least when he was with us. The situation of being divorced may have been stressful to him."

She looked, sort of slowly and wanly, at me.

"What about you? What brought you to this place?"

"My background was pretty different. My parents were refugees—their families fled Austria in the late '30s. They were both very secular. But my father, too, cared about Israel. I guess you could say in a more secular way. It wasn't 'the Jews,' it was 'the Israelis.' 'The Israelis have conquered the Sinai!' and that kind of thing. Also, in those days, there were all these mythological images coming from Israel—people picking oranges, dancing in fields, you know. It appealed to me very deeply. I guess, by the time I was a young adult, unhappily married, I reverted to those images. I was also politically intense by then, identifying with Israel a lot. But I also thought—maybe it was the subtext—that in the mythological land things might be better."

"And so ... how did you feel when you found out it wasn't a mythological land of wonders?"

I laughed.

"I adjusted pretty fast. I loved being here anyway. I don't know. It's in my bones, that this is the place to be." I said: "Even though personally I've had my *tsa'arot.*"[8]

Our eyes met.

She said: "And your parents ... what are they up to now?"

"The same. They're fine, living in Carrenden Park, retired." I said: "Your mother is—?"

She said: "My mother, you could say, is also the same. Which means, *tsa'arot.* She's still in Philadelphia. Retired. She was a schoolteacher. She remarried, but that ended too, quite a while ago. She's not that old—sixty-two, I think." She said: "My sister's in Kansas City, which is not *really* that far from Philadelphia, in this day and age, but my mother thinks it's far. If you think my mother was happy about me moving to Israel, you should think again. If you think she's happy about me moving to Australia, you should *really* think again."

I said: "Rhonda, for someone who's doing this big thing ... you don't seem overjoyed yourself."

"That's because I use you as my confessor, Andy. That's because I let you see you the dark recesses."

I said: "So you must get along pretty well with Denny. This is a pretty short time—two months?—to decide to hop across the world with someone."

She smiled. It was like seeing real sunlight—flickering—on a dark stream.

"He's so sweet. He's a really sweet guy." She said: "And it's more like three months."

"How old is he? How old are you?"

---

8 "Troubles."

"Denny is thirty-three. I am thirty-seven."

"Oh. Really?"

She looked wanly at me.

"Congratulations, Andy. You've done what everyone does when I tell them that. *Oh*?"

"It's no big deal. It's not such a big difference."

"I'm someone who looks for a daddy, and here I am with someone younger. What can I say?"

"So what are the plans for Australia?"

She seemed to sink into herself; gazed at a spot on the table.

"Big plans, Andy ... big plans." She said: "First of all, he can get me work as a shrink there. He says my American certification is fine. And ... it's all in English there."

"Great."

"And then"—she raised her eyes to mine—"if things keep working out ... and so far they're working out really well ... we're going to tie the knot."

"Wonderful." I said: "I know that sounded a bit pallid."

She broke out laughing again, brief and fierce, into her hand.

"Yeah, you didn't need a PhD in Freudian studies to know that that sounded 'pallid,' as you put it. 'Pallid.' Oh, God."

I said: "First comes love, then comes marriage, then comes ..."

She said: "Then come babies in a baby carriage."

"Babies?"

"Yup." She gave me a blue, round look. "I'm still young enough, Andy. Still young enough for two."

"Great." I said: "If things work out."

"If things work out."

"Why should you have to go to Australia to find out if things work out?"

She looked at me.

"Do I have a choice?"

"Maybe you do have a choice."

She held me in her gaze; then collapsed her forearms on the table, slumped back, gazed at a spot on the floor.

She shook her head. "No. No, Andy. Don't give me this now."

"Why not? If not now …"

She gazed at me from her slump—bright, indignant, sardonic.

"Mr. Retiree. Mr. Grandpa. Now … what? What are you saying, Andy?"

"Sometimes retirees and grandpas make mistakes. But they can correct them."

"Oh for God's sake."

She looked sideways at me.

"We haven't even been together."

"We can start."

She shook her head.

"OK. Enough. Look. I'm not going to say 'I'm not a floozy.' I *am* a floozy. Obviously. But. A floozy with limits. I do have limits."

She dabbed at her eye.

She said: "No. No. After I've been with this sweet guy, for three months, and I've promised him everything, and he's promised *me* everything. No."

"Methinks …"

We ended up saying in unison, our heads nodding: "Methinks the lady doth protest too much."

She said: "Andy, this guy is willing to go all the way with me. What are you willing to do? You've got kids, you've got a grandson, you're retired from life, what are you ready to do?"

I said: "All that's true except the 'retired from life' part." I said: "You said yourself I couldn't continue like that. So maybe you were right."

A boy, swarthy and wearing a white apron, shuffled up to our table. His eyes took in what, no doubt, looked like some sort of scene, but he showed no interest in it. He took Rhonda's empty tray and mug, then started to take my tray. I held onto my cup to signal that he shouldn't take it; there was only very little ice coffee left in it, but I didn't want there to be nothing on the table.

"What," she said—pulling up her chair again, giving me a cool, sardonic gaze, "brought about this change, may I ask?"

"Oh, I don't know … intoxicating September sunlight."

"Cut it out Lesser, I don't need your humor, OK"—laughing uncontrollably into her hand—"when I'm asking a serious question, OK?"

She was a mess—laughter, tears.

"I'm sorry, Rhonda. I mean … there's something between us, isn't there? It was there that other night too. I was just too screwed up about Hila, I don't know …"

"Oh, and you're not anymore?"

"If you'd asked me this morning if I thought anything had changed, I'd have said no. But now it's not this morning … it's now. You look nice."

"I look nice."

"Yes."

"I look nice."

"Yup."

"OK. Let me get this straight. You're willing to start all over again with your life, from the ground up, kids and everything, because I look nice. Is that it?"

"Rhonda, I'm not doing enough now. Translating isn't enough. The thought of starting all over again really doesn't bother me. I've done it before so I know what's involved. I think I'd do it better this time."

"Yeah, and what if I stop looking nice? What if I get frumpy?"

"Rhonda, there's something between us. At least it seems that way to me, maybe it doesn't to you."

"No." She raised the palms of her hands. "It seems that way to me too." She said: "You had your chance."

"Yeah, and I muffed it."

She gazed off toward the trees, shaking her head; I saw her lower lip quiver.

She said: "I think it's because I'm unattainable now, that's the whole thing. Turns out I'm with someone else, and boom … all of a sudden, *I have to have her.*"

"Rhonda, it's not that."

She said: "I wish you weren't doing this."

She pulled out her iPhone.

"I have a meeting with Esman on campus. I'm already running late."

But she kept sitting there.

I said: "You said it's still on a trial basis with Denny. So, we can be on a trial basis. But we're here."

She said: "Andy, I have devoted three months of my life to this. And I am not going to just throw it away, like a crumpled-up piece of paper, because someone gets into a mood one afternoon."

She started preparing herself to stand up.

She said: "How much was this?"

"It's all right—"

"No—"

"No Rhonda, really. I'm probably going to order something else. I'll take care of it."

She was standing. She pushed hair away from her right shoulder, adjusted her bag.

I said: "So it's ten days?"

She looked at me as if I'd said something strange and bewildering. "What?"

"You said you were going to be here for another ten days or something like that?"

"Yeah. Yeah. Something like that."

"So I guess we'll see each other."

"Yeah." She made an expressive motion. "Staircase encounters."

"Staircase encounters." I said: "That's us, I guess."

She said: "I have to go."

"Bye."

"Thanks."

"It's nothing."

"Bye."

She brushed me with a last look.

I looked at the trees, the sky.

I thought how, before, I'd been elated over a root canal that hadn't hurt. Now I had this.

# Part Three

In late October there was a breakthrough. Before that I'd been, on and off—abjectly, almost hopelessly—googling her name. It turned up almost nothing. She had a Facebook page, but it disclosed almost nothing to non-friends, and even if I'd been on Facebook myself I wouldn't, of course, have sent her a friend request. I had no intention at all of trying to make contact with her; the timing, the situation, weren't exactly appropriate. I just looked for her.

Then, one morning—still another morning of seemingly inexhaustible gentle, golden sunlight—my search turned up, as the very first result, the "Psychology Clinic Team" of the Canberra Clinical Psychology & Counselling Services site. The page gave, from top to bottom, pictures and short bios of the current seven psychologists of the clinic, and the seventh one was her. The picture—beautiful, with a mild, amiable smile—caught me up short as if I'd discovered an immense lode of gold or an answer to overwhelming questions.

The bio said:

> Psychologist Rhonda Greenspan has years of experience working with adults, couples and families, primarily in the United States. Using an interpersonal model of psychotherapy, she helps individuals change how they interact with others, leading to positive outcomes and the abatement of mental health issues. She takes a compassionate, non-judgmental approach to helping clients develop deeper insights about their difficulties.
>
> Rhonda treats depression, anxiety, stress and adjustment disorders, insomnia, relationship problems, anger and trauma, with particular attention to relationship issues. She encourages clients to develop coping strategies that enable them to live fuller and richer lives while regulating their disruptive tendencies. Rhonda seeks to gently communicate optimism to her clients, helping them to believe that change

is within our power especially when we adopt a holistically affirmative mindset.

The website gave, of course, a general email address for the clinic. I knew that I could write to it and ask to get in touch specifically with Rhonda. Again, I had no intention at all of doing so. But the discovery of the picture; of information about what was happening with her; and of even the abstract possibility of contacting her made a change. It was like being hauled to the surface and being able to breathe again.

ONE AFTERNOON, JUST about a week after the café encounter, I'd heard three diffident taps on my door. It was Rhonda.

She said: "Hi."

"Hi."

"How you doing?"

"OK."

"Yeah?"

"Yeah."

"Good. I just wanted to tell you, this is my last day here. In the building. I'm moving over to Denny's place temporarily. Then on Thursday … the big voyage."

"Oh … Want to come in?"

"Oh … no." She peered past me, as if the inside of my apartment might help her answer the question. "Thanks, but I've got the movers coming in a little while. *Balagan*."[9]

"What are you doing with all your stuff?"

"Don't ask. Big *balagan*. Some of it's going to Denny's, some of it's going to his friend so he can sell it, some of it's going to the airport. Oy. *Lahatz*."[10]

"You were able to get out of the lease?"

---

9   "A mess."

10   "Stress."

"Yeah, by forking over big bucks. I could get out of it if I paid a fine of four months' rent. So my poor landlord wouldn't be left without a tenant. He'll probably find another one in a week."

"Ha, ha."

"So," she said.

It was awkward and painful.

She said: "I have really enjoyed meeting and talking with you."

"Yeah, me too."

"I imagine ... our paths will cross."

"Yes."

I said: "Good luck over there."

"Thanks. Thanks, Andy." She said: "Bye."

"Bye."

IN THAT FIRST month after she'd left I'd sunk to a depth that surprised and perplexed me. I'd had two conversations with her of any substance. I still couldn't really say that I knew her. Yet she became all I thought about. There was, one could say, an upside: The pain over Hila drifted out the window. I was amazed, but I could almost have said that Hila was gone.

Yet the pain over Hila, at least, had made sense. I'd been with her for years; I'd wanted to keep being with her; but I'd been kicked out. Pain was a standard reaction. The pain over Rhonda made—seemingly—a lot less sense. True, it had something to do with how I'd squandered the chance; but how could I keep lashing myself over that? I hadn't been in good shape to begin with; and, of course, I still wasn't.

In that month Maayan, my daughter-in-law, kept sending me pictures and videos of Ori. She didn't realize how much good she was doing me. In about the middle of that October, I visited them in Tel Aviv. Ori was now calling me "Sab"—his version of *saba*, which means "grandfather" in Hebrew. While Maayan was getting Ori ready for bed, Yishai asked me how I was doing, and I gave him the capsule history of what had happened with Rhonda, which wasn't a long history in any case.

When I'd finished, he sat thoughtfully for a few moments.
He said: "Abba, you *have* to get back into the dating world."
I said: "Yeah, you're right. I do have to."
But I didn't.

BUT NOW I had the webpage—the webpage with her picture and bio. It became an anchor for me; as I sat translating, I not infrequently took a break to look at it yet again. I was aware that this was unhinged behavior; I was lucidly unhinged. I knew that this was a woman on the other side of the world—certainly literally, almost certainly metaphorically too. She was no longer part of my life; yet I was enshrining her. I knew it would be better if I could stop, maybe even—as Yishai had urged—return to the dating scene of real, live women. But that would be leaving her; how could I do that?

And there was a more specific reason I was attached to the page—and, particularly, looked at it in suspense the first thing each morning. It had to do with her name. Something in me was convinced that, as long as it was Greenspan, and didn't turn into Holcomb or Greenspan Holcomb, she was still "safe." Of course, this wasn't reality-congruent. If and when she married (and she may have already), she wouldn't necessarily change her last name; or she might change it but keep Greenspan as her professional name; or—eminently possible—she might change it without anyone bothering to update the webpage. All this I knew. Yet I kept checking first thing each morning and feeling relief and hope when I saw it hadn't changed.

And the webpage took on yet another significance; it became an "address," something I could write to. No, not try to write to Rhonda, the real live Rhonda, through it. But—now that even the possibility of doing that existed—I found myself writing "to her" in a different way. Basically, I found myself writing again—but not fiction, which was what I had written for decades before quitting.

Rhonda, sometimes I think it all started to go wrong back there, in that pastoral world of Carrenden Park. No, we didn't have a chance to talk about this. Our house was in the countryside, about a mile from the development where I hung out with my friends—but already far enough to be a different world, rural, almost a time warp, with a farm across the street. You looked out there and saw the cornfield and beyond it the low, squat buildings of the farm. The people plowed and hoed there and nothing changed, bright and languid in the time warp.

If you ask what a Jewish family was doing in such a place, it's a good question. There are two simple-enough answers: (1) My father, who had an MA in history from City College of New York, got a job teaching history at Schenectady County Community College; (2) my mother had always dreamed of having a sizable yard where she could plant things and cultivate them. So—anomalously in that place—strains of Schubert and Brahms wafted from our windows; it was a taste that both of my parents had picked up in their childhood in Vienna. My father, an intense intellectual, read highbrow books and journals on the living room couch in a haze of cigarette smoke. The Austro-German music from the stereo was soon joined by the sounds of my sister practicing her viola—it was all she wanted to do—hours each day. They were secular Jews, but out there in the wilderness we had Passover, we had Chanukah; we had no Christmas. Who the hell was I?

I don't want to overdramatize. I did find a social niche—among the boys—in junior high and high school. The bridge was basketball. When I became, at age twelve or thirteen, a pretty good basketball player—suddenly I was cool, suddenly I was accepted, suddenly I was liked. I had a couple of close friends and numerous buddies; I was part of the scene. But with the girls it was something else. I couldn't connect with the "goyish" girls; couldn't approach them, talk to them, much less woo them. Was this just a function of being Jewish? No; my sister, for her part, got on a lot better with the "goyish" boys and had a couple of romances with them. But still, in part, it was. I felt myself to be different from them; I felt obscure things in my depths that I both wanted and was totally unable to communicate to them …

And I kept up in that vein. Always beginning a piece by addressing it to her. Without being fully committed to what I was writing, regarding it—not so much as a draft, but as a personal, spontaneous confession to a specific listener. At the same time, I was aware that—at least in theory—something was taking shape: an autobiography. Maybe I was too young to be writing one; but I could keep adding to it, and in some more years I'd be sixty. If—hypothetically—a book, an autobiography, were to come out of it, what would be my chances, as an obscure translator, of getting it published? Not high. It would be, though, a story of *aliyah*, of Israel, so there were a few small Jewish publishers that would probably consider it. And these days, of course—though I didn't like the idea—you could self-publish.

Meanwhile I found myself returning, a few times each week, to my old, abandoned haunt—the Aroma café at the Ben-Gurion University campus—to work on it. Or not "work on it"; I refused—at this point—to let it become work, as in doing a second and third and fourth draft. No, I kept writing the segments—with pen and paper, later typing each one into a file that I did not revise—"to her." I "told" her about my hopeless yearnings for the girls I couldn't find a way to talk to, my descent into depression, mediocre schoolwork, beer-drinking, nighttime wanderings with dubious elements; about how, at basketball too, I felt that I'd failed. About how, for me, the pastoral scenery around me became a world of emptiness—most intensely in August, when all went dry and dead and the locust trilled …

About how, by the time I went to college, I was—in a way my parents weren't aware of, though my sister had inklings of it—devastated inside, with a self-conception as a desperate failure. How, when finally "a girl" appeared on the horizon, I threw myself at her, without weighing in any sort of rational way whether she was the right choice, whether her own inner problems were something I wanted or needed to contend with indefinitely into the future.

IN ISRAEL'S CLIMATE there is a phenomenon that can reasonably be called winter, with wind and rain. But throughout "winter," something that is almost spring keeps making a comeback—days of serene, lovely light without the summer heat. On one such day, in December, in the afternoon, I sat in the café on the campus. Although it had a patio with nice views of the lawns, buildings, and sky, I sat in the indoor part. The Wi-Fi worked better there, and, in addition to my iPhone, I'd brought my iPad so that—after writing—I could comfortably catch up on some news and commentary.

Amid the buzz of voices—the café was particularly full in these springlike days—I wrote about how, in my second year of college in Buffalo, at the opposite end of New York State, when I was already with Katie but not happy about it, I'd taken a creative-writing course with Professor Arno Winkler, the great critic, the white-maned famous man. About how thrilled, how enthused, how delighted he'd been with the first story I'd written for the class, something called "Another Town." In it a morose teenage boy lives in a remote rural area; it's summer, he's bored, he mopes, he looks out the window at the bright, languid cornfield and it seems to him an image of his own emptiness. One day when his mother asks him—he's recently gotten his driver's license—to drive down to the supermarket and buy some things, he willingly accedes. But somehow—even though he knows the way very well—he misses the turn to the supermarket. He finds himself driving in a rolling, verdant countryside that—strangely—doesn't seem familiar to him. He thinks the Mohawk River should be to the left, but he doesn't see it. He figures he'll drive on a little further, since it's quite pleasant here, then turn around and try to make his way back to the supermarket.

But meanwhile the countryside gets more and more pristine and beautiful. He's had a rock station playing on the radio, but there are jolts of static, which obliterate it; then slowly a sweet, orchestral music—not like anything he's ever heard before—starts filtering in. He feels a drowsiness come over him; he knows he should be concerned, but he's not … Suddenly he snaps alert; he's not aware of having fallen asleep, but it seems to have happened. Yet the car is proceeding along;

but it seems, now, to be on some kind of dirt road. Now up ahead he sees something—it looks like a small village, or a farm. And he sees people—kids his own age, guys as well as girls—standing on either side of the road. They seem to be waiting for him, waiting to welcome him …

I folded the sheets of paper and put them, and the pen, back in my knapsack; I'd tell more about it tomorrow.

My croissant was long gone but there was still coffee in my cup.

I took the iPad out of the knapsack, turned it on. It took a while to connect with the café's Wi-Fi. I tapped the email icon; it said "Checking for Mail …" for a while, seeming to ponder the possibility; then quickly hauled in five or six emails. I was particularly intrigued by one of them; it was from **Rhonda Greenspan**.

I tapped the name.

The email opened up.

I stared at it.


Andy!!


First of all, you do not know what I went through to get a hold of your email address!! You don't seem to have a website or even a Facebook page—apparently you don't need such gimmicks because you're so good that the clients just flock to you! So when searches turned out to be of no avail, I was almost going to give up and send you one of those old, ancient devices, a letter! I thought I remembered your mailbox number in "our" old building, but I wasn't sure, and wasn't crazy about the thought of sending an envelope out into the blue and just praying it would somehow find its way to you!

But before reaching that desperate stage, I remembered you telling me (during that last unlikely meeting) that you'd worked at some sort of world affairs institute at Hebrew University. I found three establishments that sort of answered to that description. Realizing that I would come off as an utter nutcase, I contacted them—actually, I called, figuring emails would quickly get consigned to oblivion. I told them I needed to get something translated from Hebrew to English, that I'd heard Andy Lesser was a good translator, that I had the impression he'd worked for them, and might they know his email address. The first two establishments indeed dismissed me as something that had escaped from the psychiatric hospital. But the third—lo!—the James Beckerman Institute of International Politics—said oh yeah, we know him, he worked here a long time ago, but he's still translating for one of our researchers, Professor Yotam Tumarkin, here's his number. And Professor Tumarkin, in a gruff way, was nice—and so Andy, here I am, much—I'm pretty sure—to your surprise.

You're probably wondering—what's going on with her down there? Why is she writing to me? Andy, it would be hard to describe to you how awful it's been since I've been here. Now, you might ask, how is it that a person like me, with my supposed professional background, did not pick up on the seriously problematic nature of Denny Holcomb while I still could have, before I traipsed halfway across the world with him (sorry but the cliché fits)? Well, one answer is wishful thinking, and the other is that I *did* pick up on it—which *you* were picking up on during our café encounter—but denied it. This is not slick psychology here, denial blah blah, it's the kind of thing that happens all the time, and yes it happens to shrinks too. Especially when, deep down, they're in kind of a desperate state. Oy gevalt.

Andy, here in Canberra, I'm eight hours ahead of you in the flow of time, meaning that it's evening. As I type to you—not having the faintest knowledge what might be happening with you, for all I know you've come out of retirement and have a harem of lovelies around you—I'm alone in my room, a glass of Cabernet on the night table beside the bed, laptop perched against my knees, sipping rather often as I type. But this is how it has been now for a few weeks—I mean, as far as wine is concerned and trying to get my mind off this awful reality.

Soon after coming here it became clear to me what was really calling Denny Holcomb back to Australia, compelling him to leave the Holy Land. It wasn't anything having to do with this nation or that nation—it was his mom. Yes, she'd been writing to him—telling him how much she missed him, imploring him to come back. Andy, don't a lot of mothers, a lot of parents of *olim*, do that? Yes. But for this *oleh* it had a special resonance. Andy, he has never broken the umbilical cord with this woman. He's still in the prenatal-bonding stage. Not long after coming here I had to realize, I had to face the fact, that being with this guy would entail competing with this woman all one's life, and of course, being doomed, at all times, to lose.

Yes, Denny is a man of his word, and he set us up quite nicely here, even before we arrived. With a nice apartment for us to live in (his family arranged it for us), and also with a nice job for me (more on that later). Well, I'm still in the apartment—but fortunately it has two bedrooms, and I've managed to secede from him, and the atmosphere between us is just businesslike now—at best—and of course it can't go on like this much longer.

Andy, I soon realized that this nice apartment we had was not "ours," it did not belong to me and Denny, but also to a third person, his mom, whose visits were very frequent and regular, basically every late afternoon! If it was just intrusiveness, one could maybe live with that, but it wasn't just that—it was an *inspection*. And who was the inspectee? You guessed it. It wasn't something overt. It was after she'd left that the criticisms would make their sinuous way to me—through her envoy, her trusted lieutenant, Denny. Andy, I am not Madame Neat and Orderly, I'm the first to admit it. But I am not *that* bad. But I was given to understand—by this team of critics—that I fell way short, that if I was planning to be the hub of a house, the matron of a couple of kids and dear Denny, I was failing drastically, I better clean up my act.

Andy, I don't want to waste too many words on this because it really isn't worth it. Suffice it to say that the criticism soon progressed beyond the mere environment I lived in, which I didn't tend to and beautify acceptably, to me myself. I didn't tend to *myself* enough. How dare I go around, in the late afternoon after work, in old jeans and a loose shirt, a bit frumpified, and not beautify myself for dear Denny, who—yes, even this was insinuated, not just by her but by him, since he basically was conjoined with his mom and endorsed every screwy, fucked-up thing she had to say (sorry)—who, if I didn't look glorious for him every second, just might check out other pastures?

It went on like that for a few weeks until I realized that it wasn't just this syndrome of his I couldn't stand, this conjoined-to-momma syndrome, but a basic trait of prissiness that is really Denny's—wherever he got it, her genes, her influence, who knows—that is really his and will keep being his if and when she leaves this earth someday (and his dad, by the way, is a nice guy and I don't know how he's tolerated this woman for so many years) and it is not something—prissy, critical, righteous, domineering—that I can live with, God forbid.

Anyway, yes, I have a nice job now at the Canberra Psychological Clinic, which Denny worked out for me because he knows people there. Most of the people are nice, I'm doing exactly what I got a degree to enable me to do, it's all in English, can't complain. And yet, when I leave this place, this apartment—soon!—I can't keep working there—because it would mean staying in Australia. And that, Andy, is something I can't do. I don't know a soul here, it's not my home. Of course, if I stayed here, I'd get to know people—actually I already have budding friendships with a couple of colleagues at work—but it simply is not my home, it is not my fate to be here. I came here on a whim, a hope, a gamble, and boy did I lose. Can't be the basis for the rest of my life—right?

So another candidate is the States. It makes sense, for sure. My mother and sister are there, and I could find work again. One problem. It's not where I want to be anymore.

And so, I don't have to explain to you what the third possibility—the only possibility—is. Guess what—I've already written to Esman, and he's willing to take me back. He meanwhile hired someone else in my stead, but he's not that good, English not that good, and while he doesn't want to boot the guy out, he'd be happy to have me on the team again too. Of course, this isn't a "solution" to anything. I think there are less than two years left to this project, and the work isn't my heart's desire in any case. I don't know, Andy. Can I get my Hebrew so it's good enough that I can work with Israeli clients? I don't think so—I started with Hebrew too late, when I was thirty, at the kibbutz. (Apart from the chants of Chaim Greenspan, which I didn't understand.) But there are a couple of places in Israel—Jerusalem, Raanana—where there are a lot of English-speaking *olim*, right? So, who knows, maybe maybe something like that could work out for me.

Meanwhile, of course, I will need somewhere to live when I make my triumphant (??) return to Be'er Sheva. I've already been in touch with a couple of apartment-owners, but they're not willing to take anyone on without meeting them in the flesh (yes, I even checked my old landlord—turned out, just as I thought, he found a new tenant right after I left!). So Andy, what I've settled on is that I'll have to stay at the Leonardo in town for a couple of weeks, and that should be enough time to find a place because they're not hard to find there. It will also be damn complicated with storing my things meanwhile and all that…but you make a (yet another) stupid mistake, like skipping off to Australia, and they come down hard on you for it, right?

And finally, Andy, I will go out on a limb—because, to repeat, I don't know what your situation is, either your inner state of mind or what you're doing—and say that I very much look forward to—I hope—seeing you again. I think about you a lot. And I've been listening to "Morning, Morgantown" on YouTube—the only thing that calms me. So idyllic. Andy, was any part of your life ever idyllic like that? I can't say that any part of mine ever was. I'm not saying it's all been terrible, of course not. But—idyllic? It seems so beautiful.

Well, Andy, I'm sorry to have plied you with such a long, prattling email—I have long needed something like this—to vent, to disclose—and I'm sorry if I've done it on your account. It's now eleven p.m. here, but you should know that in these weeks I haven't exactly been sleeping wonderfully, and if you should happen to reply, well, even in the next few hours, I may just see it in the middle of the night here Down Under. Stranger things have happened—world-embracing emails in the wee hours of night.

As always (?),

Rhonda

# Acknowledgments

The following stories have been previously published:

"She's Not Here Now" (*New English Review*)
"Thin Ice" (*IsraeLit*; and the first of the seven fictions, "The Lifeguard in Autumn," was published in *California Quarterly*)
"Two More Tries at It" (*New English Review*)
"Blind Dating in Jerusalem" (*Jewish Quarterly*)
"I'll See You There" (published as "Minimum Wage" in *Hawaii Review*)
"Sid's Blues" (*Kansas Quarterly*)
"A Little Night Musing" (*Forum*)
"Office Dreams" (*South Dakota Review*)
"Leaving the House with Hani" (*Midstream*)

# About the Author

P. DAVID HORNIK, a longtime American immigrant in Israel living in Be'er Sheva, is a writer, editor, and translator. Hundreds of his articles, mostly about Israel, have appeared in outlets like *PJ Media*, *American Spectator*, *The Times of Israel*, the *Jerusalem Post* and others, and his short stories and poetry have appeared in *New English Review*, *National Review*, *Jewish Quarterly*, *Worcester Review*, *Kansas Quarterly* and others. His published books include the essay collection *Choosing Life in Israel* and the novels *You Don't Know What Love Is* and *Beside the Still Waters*.